David Nathan was bo
been a journalist for n
ant Editor and theat
He is married with
Middlesex.

By the same author

Hancock (with Freddie Hancock)
The Freeloader
The Laughtermakers
Glenda Jackson
John Hurst, An Actor's Progress

DAVID NATHAN

The Story So Far

GRAFTON BOOKS
A Division of the Collins Publishing Group

LONDON GLASGOW
TORONTO SYDNEY AUCKLAND

Grafton Books
A Division of the Collins Publishing Group
8 Grafton Street, London W1X 3LA

A Grafton Paperback Original 1986

ISBN 0-586-06668-3

Printed and bound in Great Britain by
Collins, Glasgow

Set in Times

For Norma

Prologue

George Harper was utterly convinced that he had the right answer to the problem. The doubts of a few publicity-seeking senators, the outcry in certain cheap newspapers, the opinions of a few bleeding-heart academics, all no doubt, protestors themselves in their student days and not one of them a scientist, were at best misguided and at worst part of the general Left-wing conspiracy. There was simply no other feasible method of disposing of the 358,000 tons of defoliating chemicals, residue of the late operations in South East Asia, except by dumping it in mid-ocean. The stuff was too volatile to be burnt and, anyway, the gases so released would create a million bronchitis cases. Moreover, birds would plummet down from the skies and this, he knew, would create even more public concern. The President, a great hunter himself, would be upset by that. To break down the defoliant by chemical methods would be too costly and could only be done by the manufacturer. George knew for a fact that the manufacturing company had already approached those same officials it had bribed to over-order the stuff in the first place in an attempt to get the contract to destroy it. But it had been the President himself who had asked George Harper to, as he put it, figure out the answer and it was generally accepted that George was unbribable. There had only been one thing he had ever lusted after and that was the post of Chief Chemist to the Pentagon, and he had now been CCP for a year, ever since the last Presidential election. Also three senators had been charged with corruption as a result of a five-year FBI investigation into the original over-purchase in which specially selected female operatives had pretended to be unable to type or, in some cases, read, in order to get secretarial posts with the chief suspects. Of course it had been impossible for the FBI to penetrate the Pentagon itself in order to reach the guilty officials. Three agents who had gained entry to the Defence complex on an earlier assignment had been killed, the Defence Department pleading that they had every reason to believe from their behaviour that they were KGB men. This had raised so much doubt in the minds of the FBI chiefs that they did not press the matter further and had carefully avoided contact with the Pentagon ever since.

But then, as the Chief of Operations had put it, it wasn't as if the boys had *under*-ordered the gloop – now that would have been a very suspect act, more than likely to have been committed under the influence of foreign subversives.

No, George Harper had persuaded the President who was not, in principle, opposed to bribery as long as it was for the purpose of legitimate profit, that it was the ocean or nothing and that if a few students demonstrated against the proposal so much the better as it would then be lost in the general pattern of protest, part of the increasingly ineffective uproar against poverty, racism and other aspects of the existing social order, all of which had remained unaffected, if not more deeply entrenched by public outcry.

Anyway, once the stuff had been dumped on the spot he had selected, midway between Hawaii and the Marquesas, they would soon forget about it and turn to something else that was troubling their tender consciences. Is there no danger, the President had asked or, as he had actually put it, 'George, can I rely on you not to drop me in the shit over this?' Adding with a smile, ''Cos if you do, George, it will only be up to my knee-caps as I will be standing on your shoulders.'

George had told him: 'Mr President, Sir, perhaps in a hundred years' time, long after we've gone' – 'You George,' interrupted the President. 'Long after you've gone, George.'

' – long after I've gone,' continued George, amending seamlessly, 'and after you have retired from the Presidency, Sir, it may be, it just could be that some of the casings may break up and a few thousand square miles of plankton will die. But who'll notice it in the vastness of the Pacific except, perhaps, a few whales – and they'll be extinct by then anyway.'

'This is a serious matter, George,' corrected the President sternly, 'so cut the jokes. Have you checked this thing out thoroughly?'

'Checked it out, Sir,' said George. 'Checked it out very thoroughly. With a final check on the Pentagon computer.'

'That's good George,' said the President who never addressed a sentence to anyone without making sure he included their first name. 'Is that the same computer that had the English about to declare war on us last week?'

'They've ironed out the fault, Sir,' said George.

'All the same, George,' said the President, 'I've still got one general who wants to make a pre-emptive strike. You know I can't do that, George, not with the First Lady presently in London. How do I iron him out?'

'I also used the Yale, Harvard and MIT computers,' said George. 'They all came up with the same answer.'

He was not ignoring the President's question. He knew that the President never expected his advisers to depart from their specialist subjects. He had special advisers for that, men whose minds ranged far and wide over hundreds of different subjects and who, as they were not specialists at anything, could be safely ignored.

'And what was the answer, George?' asked the President.

'The answer was, Mr President, Sir,' said George, 'that the only possibility of anything going wrong was if the sea bed moved, that is, if there was a marine earthquake of some magnitude. All four computers confirmed that the sea bed in the selected area had remained undisturbed for 150,849 years, give or take a year or two.'

'In that case,' said the President. 'Go ahead.'

George waited.

The President added: 'George.'

A few days later six obsolete merchant vessels, accompanied by a cruiser and a pursuit vessel, slipped out of harbour early one morning just as the sun was rising.

Professor General S. V. Yakunov was despondent. The Comrade Minister was a very understanding man and knew that a scientist, unlike a writer or a politician, had to deal with facts as they were, not as they should be. Nevertheless, the Comrade Minister would require a highly detailed explanation of why, after all the exhaustive tests that had been carried out on the new fuel, it had failed to take the rocket into its planned orbit. The new fuel had been produced by the finest scientific brains in the Soviet Union, men who had brilliantly pieced together the tiny fragments of information garnered by the untiring work of the KGB's top industrial spies working ceaselessly in the West. There had been a filched laboratory report from Zurich, an indiscreet secretary in Bonn, a technical magazine article in Washington and a careless word by a French Minister unaware that his mistress had been bugged. A vital clue had been provided, albeit unknowingly, by a long-serving KGB mole in a rubber goods factory in Watford on the outskirts of London. He had photographed an order for a gossamer with specifications that combined strength and sheerness unknown to Soviet technology. When it had been successfully reproduced, with the help of a Japanese professor of chemistry, blackmailed into subservience through a disastrous affection for a repellent but photogenic Yokohama transvestite, also in the pay of the KGB, a particularly high-flying newly-graduated student from the Piyatagorsk Institute of Higher Technology had realized that it was the first substance ever invented that was capable of containing more energy than it had mass and that, therefore, if volatilized, it would revolutionize current concepts of fuel injection systems.

All this, thought Professor General Yakunov bitterly, is now gone to waste simply because I will not be able to answer the Comrade Minister's reasonable enough question – why has it failed? All had seemed well at first. The new rocket fuel had functioned perfectly and the rocket had risen, majestically phallic in its shape and thrust, symbol of Soviet might and irresistible advanced technology. Then, with the despairing suddenness of a premature ejaculation, it had lost impetus, flopped nose downward and plunged, at 14,000 miles an hour, into the ocean.

Professor General Yakunov shook his head as if to shake it free of the sexual symbolism. A rocket is a rocket and a penis is a penis, he told himself firmly. And the one had nothing at all to do with the other. On the other hand, they did look alike, sometimes. Nowadays, sexual imagery frequently entered his mind unbidden and he was sure it was affecting his work. Yet how could it? There were no females in the computer room where he spent most of his time. No males either. Just him and the computer. So how could there be any influences of a sexual nature? The idea was absurd. No, the only thing he loved was the computer itself. Its sheer elegance fascinated him; the rounded contours of the discs, the throbbing pulsations of the inner circuits as they reacted instantly to the touch of his hands as he lightly caressed the console keys, all gave him a deep joy. Above all, though, it was the computer's capacity for instant and full response that never ceased to thrill him. Professor General Mrs Yakunov was never like that, sighed Professor General Yakunov. How he and the computer would have enjoyed analysing the constant flow of reports received from all the equipment carried in the rocket! Now all was silence except for one faint signal whispering up from the depths, one needle still flickering among the stilled bank of dials that had, only a few seconds before, danced and trembled before him with their coded messages. With the help of this last weakly pulsating tremor, they could locate the exact spot where the main body of the rocket lay. But to what purpose? They could not salvage it. If only they had the advanced underwater salvage equipment the Americans possessed it might be possible, but they hadn't. Professor General Yakunov cursed himself for a fool. Of course the Americans must have tracked the rocket, must be aware that it had failed, knew precisely the spot where it had plunged to the ocean floor and even now were picking up the same death rattle from its instrument panel. American nuclear submarines would be racing towards the spot, would stand guard over his stricken rocket while the special salvage equipment sped to the rendezvous. Professor General Yakunov's hand reached out to the button marked 'DESTRUCT'. He pressed it firmly. The electric impulse flashed half-way round the world, penetrated a mile-deep blanket of water and the life in the needle was snuffed out.

When the big fish started floating to the surface and the sea took on a yellowish tinge and frothed even in a flat calm and reports came in of drifting fishing boats crewed by corpses, George Harper kissed his wife Mildred and his daughter Pansy goodbye and set off to sea. Whatever was the cause of these incidents, he told journalists at a press conference hastily arranged at the White House, it was not the chemical defoliant. It was known, he said, that the Russian rocket that had fallen in the area, that had deliberately been destroyed, was using a new kind of fuel. God alone knew what noxious mixture the Commies had concocted. This was most likely the cause of the trouble, if trouble there was and it was not all an invention or, at the very least, an exaggeration created by the international forces that were ready and willing to jump on to any bandwagon that was critical of the American Government and from which not even that great human being, the President himself, was exempt.

The President himself called George into the Oval Office and said, the smile on his face as crinkly and as warm as ever, 'I'm only going to say one thing, George, and even that is not new. On your shoulders George.'

George looked blank. The President enlarged. 'I'll be standing on your shoulders, George, like I said.'

When he came out a stray reporter accosted him. 'What did the President say?' he asked. 'Only that I have the full weight of his support,' said George.

When the USS Idaho reached the spot where, according to the navigation officer, the ships containing the defoliant had been scuttled a few weeks before, his assurances were superfluous. An untrained eye could see that the ocean did, in fact, have a yellowish tinge and an inexperienced nose could not fail to detect the stench of decaying fish that rolled sluggishly in the flat calm as if there were still some slow pulsations of life beneath the dulled scales or at the extremities of the drifting tentacles. George Harper examined the scene with the eyes of the trained scientific observer and concluded that his best course was to analyse some of the liquid in which the vessel and its escorting flotilla of putrefying flesh drifted and he made the necessary requests. The bottles containing the liquid were duly delivered to him in the makeshift laboratory deep in the bowels of the vessel and he began work.

That night, George Harper paced up and down the deserted deck and pondered on the findings he had made. Certainly the Russian explosion must have blown to shreds the protective casings around the chemical warheads, had, in fact, set off the explosive charges they had contained in order to maximize the scatter effect. The sea was, therefore, heavily contaminated. But far more so than the mere release of the defoliant would have indicated. Something else had happened; something else had mixed with the defoliant to make it more virulent and powerful than he had conceived to be possible. Clearly, the rocket's fuel tanks had ruptured and, whatever they were using, when combined with the defoliant and, possibly exacerbated instead of adulterated by contact with sea water, would change the face of chemical warfare. He was on the verge of a great discovery. His name would go down alongside Kreplach and his new paralysing gases, Wintringham and his auto-destructive bubonic bacteria which spread plague and then devoured itself before the occupation troops arrived on the scene and Von Blintz with his odourless, tasteless, rapid-ageing compound which could turn an army of young men into doddering, tottering ancients within a few days of it being introduced into their water supply. George Harper's name was similarly assured of immortality. There would be a Congressional Medal of Honour in it for him and, if things really went well, a counter-organization that would make the anti-nuclear lobby look like a PTA protest meeting. Of course, the NASA boys would want some samples so that they could isolate the fuel ingredient, but that was a secondary matter. The main thing was to get more of the stuff and take it back to his laboratory in the Pentagon as quickly as possible. It needed far more sophisticated equipment than was available on board the Idaho.

He had used all the samples the crew had obtained for him but there was just one more test he wanted to carry out before turning in. He would get it himself. He tied a piece of string around the neck of a glass beaker and lowered it over the side into the dark, oily water in which the froth now glowed, faintly phosphorescent. It was further than he thought. The bottom of the beaker just touched the surface of the water. A few inches more was all he needed. He leaned further forward, strained – and fell. He yelled as he felt himself lose his balance and surfaced spluttering. Once he had got over the initial shock it was not unpleasant. The water was warm and there was no current. He splashed about by the side of the huge ship making the phosphorescence dance in the moonlight. He could see his fall had not gone unnoticed. A lifebelt thudded into the sea a yard from him and he reached out to grasp it. A rope ladder was thrown over the side. He could see preparations being made to lower a boat. He shouted that he was all right and, letting go of the lifebelt, pulled himself up the ladder. As he reached the top, willing hands helped him over the rail.

'I'm all right, I'm all right,' George Harper reiterated as his feet touched the deck. 'It was just a silly accident. I'll be quite all right,' he assured the solicitous sailors and then he dropped dead.

The sailors stood in a circle looking at the corpse as it slowly turned grey and started to shrivel. Those who had touched George and had been splashed by sea water rushed away to wash. The others brought a fork-lift truck and carefully lifted the body into one of the regulation navy coffins and reverently placed it in the ship's deep freeze. Then they sailed for home.

The Pentagon gave George Harper a burial with full honours, General Kirk Czsyklowski, commanding general of the Chemical Division making a moving speech in which he said that George Harper had died, like so many brave chemists before him, in defence of the free world and for the greater benefit of mankind. Before he strode to his waiting car he placed one arm around Mrs Harper's heaving shoulders and the other around Pansy who was fourteen but looked older and said that he had meant every word he said. Then, giving Pansy one last squeeze of solace, he strode off manfully.

'Oh Pansy,' sobbed Mrs Harper. 'It was so beautiful.'

A leaf fluttered down from one of the noble trees that guarded the graves. 'Your father would so much have appreciated all that was said about him.' A gust of wind blew down more leaves on to the two black-clad mourners and swirled among the uniforms of the military men who, in many cases, were accompanied by their wives or secretaries. Some of the leaves settled on the raw clay by the side of the grave and some fluttered down into the grave itself.

'I always feel,' said Mrs Harper, wiping away a tear, 'that funerals are even sadder in the Fall when the trees start to shed their leaves. It's kind of, well, symbolic, isn't it Pansy. I'm sure you are old enough to understand these things now.'

'But Mother,' said Pansy. 'It is only June.'

A week later every tree in the cemetery was dead. So was the grass. Everything had shrivelled and turned grey.

Harold Prendergast's London rose higher and higher. His tower blocks dominated every horizon, vertical villages teeming with people, cellular structures which swayed gently in the wind and caused aircraft to be re-routed. In Prendergast the times had found their man. His passion for building high coincided with the nation's need for more and more living space. When Prendergast perfected his lighter, stronger, pre-stressed, pre-fabricated concrete cubes and then demonstrated that he could erect tower blocks faster and cheaper than anyone else, desperate local authorities fought for his services. 'The sky,' he was fond of saying, 'is not the limit.'

In a few years the chronic housing shortage which had defeated successive governments of both parties and numerous political attitudes, was virtually over. With production-line precision the inhabitants of slum houses, of gaunt Victorian villas, sub-divided into seven-to-a-room tenancies, of decaying 19th century blocks stinking with seeping sewage, were hustled into their new aerial environment and their festering old quarters demolished within days, sometimes hours, of their leaving them, in order to make way for yet more Prendergast blocks.

The people were grateful. They came out of their bug-infested, rat-haunted hovels and rose in grey, plastic-walled lifts to sterilized concrete cubes to marvel at the washing-machine fitted kitchens, the wipe-clean walls and all the incorporated labour-saving devices the prodigious Prendergast had ingeniously crammed in. They moved, as if in a dream of happiness, to look out on views of unsurpassed splendour. The domes of St Paul's and the Old Bailey pimpled beneath them in the haze and the only proportionate objects in the whole vast and windy landscape were other Prendergast towers. It was at this point that a great many of them vomited.

However, they moved in because they had no other choice and, while a number of inquisitive children were killed through making too-large an exploration of too-small a balcony, this was, as Prendergast said when interviewed on the mortality rate, no greater than those who were formerly killed by motor cars while playing in the streets or who had contracted virulent diseases owing to the unhygienic conditions in which they had once lived.

Criticism that the new blocks were soulless was contemptuously dismissed by Prendergast who, with some justice, asked if there had been much evidence of soul in the old slums. He would then point out on the faintly colour-washed drawings that decorated his office the pedestrian precincts with which each block was surrounded, pleasant concrete-lined walks making interesting and artistic patterns of curves, slopes and ramps. Even the tenant who appeared on a television programme and said that he would not be seen dead in Prendergast's pedestrian precinct was proved wrong a few days later when he fell into it from his 52nd floor balcony.

More difficult to counter were reports of a number of housewives found cowering in the corner furthest away from the windows, or who sat all day with the curtains drawn or who tried to persuade their husbands – often with some success – to board or brick up every window. In this way the sufferers from vertigo were able to cope with their new situation until, as usually happened, they contracted claustrophobia as well. There were other, less easily identifiable disorders. One diagnosed by psychiatrists as zephrophobia or fear of winds was characterized by an irresistible urge to shelter in shop doorways or a refusal to leave a building in anything stronger than a Force 2 breeze. There was a general increase in drug-taking, both official and unofficial, alcoholism, violence, suicide and twitching. Large numbers of children, brought up in flats more than thirty storeys high, were classed as ineducable because when placed at or about ground level they simply stared vacantly into space and rocked to and fro, their arms crossed on their chests, their hands holding opposite shoulders.

In answer to complaints of this nature, a spokesperson for the Combined London Authorities said: 'Some people are never satisfied.'

Long before Prendergast, the hospitals, mental asylums and psychiatric clinics had been unable to cope with the increasing number of patients requiring treatment, but now the strain was so great that the psychiatrists and nurses were themselves breaking under it. Fortunately, however, the authorities, at long last freed from the task of building houses, had sufficient resources to enable them to provide new hospitals, lunatic asylums and clinics. These were quickly erected and equipped with the latest scientific equipment for blasting people back into normality or, to give it a more scientific term, docility, but the problem of finding space for these community services as they came to be called became acute and eventually Prendergast, the man who had achieved one miracle, was called in to perform another. He studied the problem for a considerable time and eventually came up with a plan for neighbourhood conglomerates, each one comprising a hospital, psychiatric clinic, lunatic asylum and high security area so that a patient could be processed with minimum bureaucracy from one to the other as his needs developed. With a whole floor reserved for different aspects of mental illness ranging from mild anxiety to raging psychosis the buildings would surpass any existing structure by at least ten storeys.

The authorities turned the plan down. Even they could see that treating patients with vertigo and other height-induced conditions, 1,000 feet above ground level, would pose difficulties that psychiatry, despite recent major advances, would be unable to surmount.

This was Prendergast's first real rebuff, the first setback in his long and glittering career. It was not to be his last. It became noticeable that the concrete facing on the first Prendergast Projects was beginning to flake heavily. Tenants on the topmost floors claimed that the amount of sway had increased appreciably and, though at first their worries were dismissed as mere imagination, their fears seemed to be confirmed when an enterprising newspaper engaged a civil engineer of formidable reputation to take some measurements. He reported that in high winds the movement of the building he had tested was several centimetres more than the regulations allowed.

Prendergast replied that even if this were so it was well within tolerable limits. At the same time he took the opportunity of scoffing at insinuations that his buildings were suffering from concrete fatigue. 'There is,' he said, 'no such thing as concrete fatigue – at least, not in my concrete.'

To prove his total confidence in his work he and his beautiful Scandinavian wife, a statuesque blonde who had been devoted to him for twenty years, took up residence in a small flat on top of Prendergast Project One, the very first block he had ever built. They were pictured by television newsreel cameras and all the newspapers, she towering over the stove in the tiny kitchen, he enjoying the extensive view from the balcony. That night, Prendergast felt a pronounced and powerful surge of sexual energy and began to make love to his wife with a violence and force that sent her mind reeling back to the early days of their marriage. Her friends had said that no 4 ft 6 ins midget, as Prendergast was, could ever satisfy her but she had felt the power that lay within the man, sensed the enormous forces bottled up in that small but burly frame. And she had been right. He had given her a son as tall and as well-made as she was and she had never felt the need even to look at another man, much less consider him as a potentially more satisfactory lover than her husband. And now, here again, was the indescribable pleasure of seemingly being able to feel the whole man – not just part of him – within her, even though, at the same time, she was aware of his head on her breast and his toes hammering against the inside of her right thigh. The new surroundings inspired Harold to a transcendental sexuality. She responded to his ardour as she had always done, straining to envelop him in the folds of her still strong flesh, arching upwards to meet this insistent driving force that was transporting her with delight, that was making the whole world tilt, that was creating in her ears the sweetest thunder she had ever heard.

When the dust settled on what was left of Prendergast Project One, Harold Prendergast and his wife were found near the top of the huge mound of rubble locked in each other's arms. Some 1,400 others perished with them. It was the same with the three other blocks which collapsed while plans to evacuate them were being discussed. The official report, nine months later, by the Government Committee of Inquiry, said that there was some evidence that an unusual amount of celebrations involving much singing and dancing took place on hearing the news of the collapse of Project One and the death of Harold Prendergast. This had largely contributed to the disasters involving Projects Two, Three and Four.

Prendergast and Harper both died on the same day. Neither had ever heard of the other, but each, in his own way, was an important figure in the mid-sixties.

A few months after her father's death Pansy Harper decided that it was high time that she did something about the revolution. They had been demonstrating and talking for such a long time that the early stages of protest were now the subject of fond reminiscences by elderly people such as her forty-year old English master who could easily be sidetracked into recalling the freedom marches and the battles against the fuzz and the peace demos. But the rich were still rich and the poor were still poor, if not poorer, and the black man was still exploited even if, in some cases, the exploiters were other black men, and men were still oppressing women and what's more she was still a virgin at fifteen and something had to be done about every one of these things.

Pansy took to the road and a passing motorist who said

that he had a daughter at home just like her and it was important for him to know what the young were thinking about and it was easier to talk to a comparative stranger about, well, er, intimate things, than it was to his own children, wasn't it and didn't she find it easier to talk to him than her own father. Yes, said Pansy. Good, said the motorist, it was best to be perfectly frank and open and had she had many sexual experiences? Not, said Pansy, as many as she wished she'd had. And she inquired of the now perspiring motorist if he wished to make love to her. 'You're quite some kid,' he said. 'Because if you are,' continued Pansy, 'we are just about to cross the state border into Virginia and if you have an immoral purpose you had better do it now otherwise there could be complications.'

'Like hell,' said the motorist. 'On the main highway? With a car passing every three seconds, police patrols every mile and clearway no stopping signs every few yards. Are you crazy?'

However, he stopped the car long enough to throw her out of it.

On reaching San Francisco, Pansy found a commune and had several intense and beautiful experiences with folk singers of both sexes before settling down with a young black militant. When he moved on to take up a place at the Harvard Business School she was, for a time, at a loose end. As a girl brought up in the shadow of the Pentagon she was, of course, of vague revolutionary tendencies so she joined the People's Democracy Party which had been founded by Professor Darius Deering. There were very few other members as some of the certainty had gone out of things, the Professor having reached a personal crisis in his political credo.

'We seem,' he told Pansy in one of their increasingly personal seminars, 'currently to be at an interface between two imperatives of the human condition, both having the same or similar purpose, that is, a general belief in the necessity of creating optimum favourable conditions for the continuation of the human species. This can be done in one of two ways, broadly speaking, that is. The first is the continuation of the capitalistic ethic which, briefly, is that every man is for himself and the devil takes the hindmost. This is believed by those who practice it to be the best way to ensure the future of the human race as represented by them and their immediate family. If everybody did as they do, the argument runs, everyone would have more than enough for their needs. The in-built fallacy is that if everybody insisted on and possessed the power to impose their economic will on the community in order to safeguard their own interests there would be insufficient material goods to go round. Accordingly it becomes manifest that the only way to protect themselves and their friends and families is to band together in order to create, maintain or increase their power. In this way they abandon, if they ever possessed, the concept of working for the good of humanity as a whole and, instead, narrow down their area of concern first to the nation state they inhabit – especially at a time of external threat – and, when the danger comes from within, to the social class to which they belong, that is people who hold similar positions or have similar possessions.'

'Down with the capitalist pigs,' said Pansy.

'The other method,' continued Professor Deering, ignoring her, 'is the broad socialist principle of one for all and all for one, a perfectly acceptable slogan for capitalists when applied to the sports- or battle-field but intolerable in a wider area for it means the strong helping the weak and, even more alarmingly, the rich helping the poor. It means co-operating instead of competing, it means the long-term planning of resources for the benefit of all instead of squandering them on the most profitable short-term enterprise. It means the brotherhood of man instead of the law of the jungle. It is a more noble concept than capitalism, a vision of a classless society of equality, freedom and sufficiency.'

'Right on man,' said Pansy.

'Unfortunately,' continued Professor Deering, 'its inbuilt fallacy is that it is predicated on the view that humanity is made up of the innately good and the inherently sensible and both of these concepts are contradicted by the prevalence of capitalists in every society where they have even the most minimal conditions for practising the business of buying at one price and selling at another, even where there is not all that much to buy and sell in the first place. Plus the fact that whatever part of the world you look at, people are trying to get out of the so-called socialist countries to start life afresh among the evils of capitalism. Sometimes they risk death or long periods of imprisonment; sometimes they accept parting for long periods from people they care deeply about, sometimes they know they will suffer hardship and the loneliness of being in a country where a foreign tongue is spoken. And there is no traffic in the other direction.'

And the Professor sighed deeply.

Pansy immediately perceived her mission. Here was this poor man trapped in – what did he call it? – an interface, caught between two political poles, floundering between the capitalist devil and the deep red sea. No wonder she was the only person at the Professor's seminars. Leaders could not be doubters; they had to express an unwavering conviction, a steadfast confidence that they had the answer, knew the truth, held the key. Professor Deering had to be forced to make a firm stand on one side or the other. But which? There he hovered like a baffled bee between two flowers. It was her task to guide him to one or the other. Which would it be, capitalism or socialism? Deep inside she knew there was a personal issue as well; knew that if she pulled it off and reinvigorated Darius Deering with a new belief in himself as a political leader there would follow a belief in her, a need for her. So which would it be? For Pansy there could be no doubt. Capitalism meant the status quo in America. What was the point of being a confirmed capitalist in a capitalist country? 'How,' she cried, 'can you talk about the failure of socialism when socialism has never been tried? Is Russia a socialist country? No. Is China? No.'

'You may be right,' said Deering, hesitantly, 'all the same there are a lot of variations – Jugoslav socialism, Albanian socialism, French socialism, English socialism . . .'

'English socialism?' interrupted Pansy. 'What's that?'

'Between 1945 and 1979,' said Professor Deering, 'Britain had a socialist government for most of the time.'

'I never knew that,' said Pansy, marvelling once again at the Professor's breadth of knowledge. 'What have they got now?'

'It's difficult to say,' said the Professor. 'Something called the mixed economy. Whatever it is it doesn't work very well. But then,' he sighed, 'nothing does. Every system that has been tried in any place and at any time has always resulted in both economic and social injustice for most of the people most of the time. Oh it may be that for a brief period after a new party has achieved office the ideals that fired it in the first place are maintained. For a little while compassion for the underdog, the weak, the poor, the dispossessed flowers and their condition is ameliorated slightly. But the imperatives of power always reassert themselves and the planned programme is abandoned. At best the new leaders adopt the policies that the discredited old leaders muddled through and at worst the recently-emptied prisons are refilled with new victims accused of the same old crimes of being anti-State or even anti-God. The executioners are reinstated and Bullwhip Goldberg rides again.'

'Who – ' Pansy began.

'Bullwhip Goldberg,' said Professor Deering, who knew a feed line when he uttered one, 'was the chief of police of Soncino City, a small town in California in the early 'seventies. On the outskirts of town was an encampment of radicals of all complexions – anarchists, hippies, yippies, socialists, macrobiologists, you know the kind of thing, guitar players and folk-singers, gays, nose-flute players, makers of junk jewellery, leather belts, fat coloured candles and collages of sea shells. Every now and then some of them wandered into town, usually with a stark naked runny-nosed kid strapped to their backs, while the women tried to sell some junk so that they could get some dough to buy some junk. Naturally, this kind of thing upset the good people of Soncino City and Bullwhip Goldberg, the local sheriff, picked up their feelings without even having to have them uttered into his pearly fat-lobed ears. Hustling and bullying and shoving these radicals around just naturally appealed to him and he did everything he was empowered to do by way of the various statutes and bye-laws regarding vagrancy and indecency and a great deal he was not empowered to by any law whatsoever, legal, moral, natural or jungle. The good citizens of Soncino City watched with pleasure as he harried and hustled and bullied these, for want of a better word, radicals until they mainly remained in their encampment just outside the city's boundaries and only occasionally crept into the nearest supermarket on the outskirts of town in order to get some necessity such as deep frozen giant prawns. The less they saw of those radicals, as they called them, the more the people of Soncino City worried about them. What were they doing out there? What sneaky thing were they up to. They transmitted their fears to Bullwhip Goldberg and he said the good folks were not to worry, he'd run those pinko commies right out of town. "How can you do that, Bullwhip," asked one more than usually acute citizen. "They ain't in town." This baffled Bullwhip for a time but he wasn't Chief of Police only because he knew some dirt about the mayor. "This is what we do," he told another meeting six months later. "We extend the town's boundaries to include the encampment – and *then* we run them out." This plan was greeted with roars of acclaim by the assembly and the town council went into immediate session to pass the necessary resolution. The mayor congratulated Bullwhip on his scheme. "With the election coming up in a couple of weeks," he said, "this will just about clinch things. Nothing to worry about, eh, Bullwhip?" The next day, Bullwhip went out to the encampment with a legal piece of paper clutched in one massive hand, his bullwhip, of course, in the other. He was a little surprised to see how the encampment had grown for, being forced back on their own resources, they had all written home for money and now there were some sizeable businesses flourishing for where there's a need there's a store. Bullwhip was also surprised at the large crowd that turned out to greet him so, averting his eyes from the ground and keeping them firmly fixed on the outlines of the bra-less breasts beneath the thin blouses of the women, he stated his business, telling them that (a) they were now in town and (b) they'd better get out of it. But quick. "How long have we got?" inquired one fair-haired youth. "Till sundown," snarled Bullwhip. "Good," said the young man, "that will give me plenty of time to get an injunction." Bullwhip blenched. If there was one thing he was afraid of it was a smart-arsed lawyer. "Now don't you go threatening me with the law," he roared. "I'm the law in these parts." "You used the law to extend the town's boundaries," said the young man. "It's only right that we should use it to gain a little time. We've got a lot of property and goods to shift here."

'The word "property" was kinda sacred to Bullwhip and the word "injunction" made him uneasy so he said, "How long do you want kid?"

'"Would two weeks be all right?" asked the youth politely.

'Bullwhip considered. That would make it the day after the election. It would be a good start to the mayor's new term for the townsfolk to see all these long-haired kids winding their way out of the area with their naked kids and screwy clothes. "Okay," he said. "Two weeks it is. And not a day more."

'"Thank you," said the fair-haired young man.

'Bullwhip turned round and was striding purposefully back to his car when the fair-haired youth called him. "Mr Bullwhip," said the youth. "What now?" snarled Bullwhip, turning in his tracks. "I got to understand you right, this place is now part of the town huh?" "It sure is," said Bullwhip. "Cast-iron-water-tight. Governor McCoy signed the paper yesterday." "In that case," said the youth, "seeing as we live here, we must be citizens, yes?"

'Bullwhip knotted his forehead. Citizens? Just because you lived in a city didn't make you a citizen, did it? Or did it? "Citizens?" he said. "I don't know about that," said Bullwhip in the quietest voice anyone had ever heard him use. "I guess I'll have to ask the Mayor."

'"At the same time," said the youth, "will you inquire about a voting station for this area and tell him that I will be standing for the office of Mayor."

'On the way back to town – or rather, the older part of town – Bullwhip broke the speed law three times over. Of course the youth won, there being more radicals in the town by then than solid straight citizens and the first thing the kid did was to sack Bullwhip as Chief of Police. Bullwhip couldn't do anything about it as he knew nothing to the boy's detriment.'

'But,' said Pansy, 'you said – '

'I said Bullwhip Goldberg rides again,' said the Professor, who knew an unfinished story when he told one. 'And that's just what happened. The new town legislature passed ordinances giving free lunches and free transport to schoolkids and old people, started a programme of public works to solve the town's unemployment problem, increased social security benefits for those who still could not be absorbed and opened an abortion clinic. Now all this not only horrified the grey suits but put up their tax bills as well. They started protest meetings and at one of them they got a little excited and marched down to City Hall where they began to demonstrate. Things started to get out of hand. Someone threw a brick which smashed a window in the chamber where the new council was debating not if but when they should start the free legal and medical services. The councillors were furious. Here they were, a legally-elected, democratically-chosen body whose deliberations were being prevented by the hooligan mob outside. Where, they asked, was the new Chief of Police?

'The new Chief of Police was fully aware of his duties. "I'm going out there now to sort this thing out," he said firmly. And so he did – went out there, that is. He stood on the balcony and faced the now raging mob. "Peace," he said, making the sign. "Peace and love." Moments later he was felled by a stone thrown by a short-haired, grey-suited man wearing both a collar and a tie. The news was brought to the chamber by an ashen-faced aide. The councillors were aghast, bewildered. At that moment there was a knock on the door. Bullwhip Goldberg stood there, huge and solid. "I guess you folks need me," he said. Quickly, they appointed him Chief of Police in place of the late incumbent and he immediately went into action. He cracked six skulls and packed the town jail with the dozen people nearest to it. The riot dispersed. As he explained to the new mayor over a cup of coffee the following morning, "You are now the duly constituted authority of this town," and he added in an uncharacteristic outburst of candour, "whether the skulls I crack are covered in short hair or long hair doesn't matter, just as long as I'm doing the job I was cut out for."'

For the most part Pansy had listened to the tale of Bullwhip Goldberg in silence, coming in only on what were intentional cues. Now she said, 'But at least the poor, the sick, the old and the unemployed had some benefits out of the new regime.'

'Not for long,' said the Professor. 'The banks didn't like it so they pressed for repayment of town loans and refused to extend any more credit. This meant that more money had to be raised by local taxation. Only by now it wasn't only the old business people of the town who objected but the new ones. All the old sellers of jewellery, sea-shells, leather belts and coloured candles were only selling that kind of stuff because they didn't have the capital to buy the kind of thing they really wanted to sell like motor cars and Hershey bars and shirts and underpants and deep frozen country fresh oven-ready chickens.

'Once they were able to get proper premises and raise money at the banks they settled down and, in some cases, had hair cuts and wore bras except at weekends. They didn't like paying heavy taxes any more than anyone else so by the time the next election came round the fair-haired youth had to promise to introduce "sensible" policies or inevitably lose. As all his old supporters still called themselves radicals most of them voted for him but it was clear that he would lose power eventually if he didn't close the abortion clinic, cut down the public works, refuse to pay for the free legal and medical services and cut out the free transport and lunches for the young and old.'

'But if he couldn't do anything why should he want to cling on to the office?' asked Pansy.

'Ah,' said the Professor, 'because the office is power or at least has the trappings of power and you must be familiar with Acton's dictum.'

'Acton's dictum?' wondered Pansy out loud.

'All power corrupts and absolute power corrupts absolutely. It is something everyone quotes and everyone agrees with and no one does anything about.'

'So why don't you?' asked Pansy.

'To do something about it,' explained the Professor patiently, 'you would need to seek power. No doubt you can spot the inherent contradiction.'

'You have old-fashioned ideas,' said Pansy.

'I'm supposed to be a very advanced thinker,' said the Professor.

'So advanced,' said Pansy, 'that we're far out in front of everyone else. That explains why there's no one here except me.'

'They want solutions,' said the Professor, 'and I can only give them problems.'

'You can give them more than that,' said Pansy. 'You can give them the solution that you have arrived at, which has been staring you in the face.'

'Only you have been staring me in the face for the last hour or two,' said the Professor, 'and you look more like a problem to me.'

'I may be,' said Pansy, 'in fact, I'm determined to be, but that's not what I meant. What I meant was that what the world needs is an anti-power party, a party that will analyse where the power lies in any society and immediately press for legislation to curb it. If the power lies with big business it will support the unions, if it's with the unions, it will support – '

'Support big business?' asked the Professor.

'Why not, if that's the logic of the situation? It has to be flexible, undogmatic, its sole purpose to work for the diminution of power whoever possesses it, whether it's the state or the individual.'

'We'll be flooded with anarchists,' said the Professor, 'and there's nothing more tedious.'

'No we won't. We're not against government or power. Someone should be doing something somewhere, at some time. We just want to curb their power, that's all.'

'You mean you want weak government,' said the Professor.

'Sure,' said Pansy. 'Weak government must be better than strong government. It makes them take notice of what people think.'

'I have only one more thing to ask,' said the Professor, 'before closing this seminar. Will you marry me?'

'No,' said Pansy, 'but I'll come and live with you.'

A month after he had published a paper outlining his ideas for the Flexible Party, ready to oppose any and every identifiable power centre, social, economic or political, Professor Deering was invited to take up the post of Professor of Social Engineering at an English university. He accepted with alacrity.

When Harold Prendergast and his wife were safely covered with dust for the second and final time, their son Arthur returned to his university to resume his state-aided studies into the best methods of overturning the state. He read and frequently quoted the sayings of Chairman Mao who, at that time, was still considered to be a Person of Some Consequence in China and elsewhere. He organized a raid on the vice-chancellor's files as a result of which a strong statement was issued condemning the fascist practice of classifying students according to their sex and intelligence, took his clothes off in the main street of the town as a mark of protest against bourgeois concepts and threw a pot of paint over a visiting politician in defence of free speech. He was finally sent down for telling a proctor to fuck off.

He made for London where he joined the National Revolutionary Committee which aimed to bring about the rule of the people by ending the tyranny of the ballot box. The committee was open to anyone who cared to join and had several thousand members, in fact everyone who belonged to the National Revolutionary Party. The committee's programme and activities were arranged by a democratically-elected sub-committee of five headed by George Hood-Phillips, its founder. Hood-Phillips had established his radical reputation when a lecturer by leading his students out of the campus and on to the picket lines in an act of solidarity with local motor car workers. Angered at what they conceived to be a waste of tax-payers' money the car workers attacked the students, seized their banners proclaiming student-worker solidarity and inflicted injuries severe enough to send four of them to hospital. Thus confirmed in his views that a stronger relationship between worker and intellectual was the most urgent priority of the time, Hood-Phillips had formed the National Revolutionary Party and its all-embracing committee. This quickly attracted such activists as the Reverend Hilary Jones whose book, 'The New Trinity', was considered to be the classic synthesis of Marxist-Maoist-Christian thought, Ben Shepherd, the shop steward who, since he gained his Open University BA had been in great demand by university debating societies, Isidore X, the West Indian leader of AW! (the Annihilate Whitey Movement), and the lovely Clementina Carstairs, the actress, in whom passion and principles had so coalesced as to produce a radiance that was irresistible to all but the most right-wing audiences.

The sending down of Arthur Prendergast, who was

immediately co-opted on to the sub-committee, was the signal for a series of demonstrations, protest marches, sit-ins and student strikes, all defending Arthur's right of free expression regarding proctors or anyone else. Anyone who attempted to put the case for Arthur's dismissal went unheard, his arguments being drowned by chants of 'Free Speech!' Clementina, being between pictures and stage engagements, took an active role in all these activities, marching bravely and beautifully, her long golden hair catching every camera lens, in the midst of every melée. She remained unbloodied as if by a miracle, the police having been given strict orders that in no circumstances must she be clubbed down or marked in any way.

Naturally, Clementina and Arthur, who had inherited his father's fondness for tall blonde ladies, grew fond of each other and their relationship continued even after the Prendergast Cause, as it had become known, was superseded by more urgent social injustices such as unemployment, nuclear disarmament, racism and abortion rights. It was one of the great political discoveries of the time that all these separate issues, each with its own complex causes, were considered to be susceptible to amelioration by the simple process of standing in the street in large numbers and shouting in unison.

Whenever Clementina was in England between film locations she stayed at Arthur's flat as it was more convenient than her own and, she had to admit, more comfortable. Arthur had been left a great fortune by the sudden death of his parents and lived in some splendour. He disposed of interviewers who drew attention to his lifestyle and the fact that he had no need to work for a living by pointing out that neither did he have a need – in the sense that they used the term – to work for revolution either. Clementina realized that she loved Arthur when she made the great sacrifice and accepted a part in a

West End production at £1,000 a week in order to be near him. The couple were regarded by all sections of society as inseparable and it was little surprise to anybody when they announced the birth of a son in the Out of Wedlock column in The Times. They were going to call the child Mao Carstairs-Prendergast until someone pointed out the initials MCP would not be suitable for the offspring of such advanced parents. They therefore dropped the Carstairs for which Clementina, vaguely uneasy about performing the role of mother, was relieved, and toyed with the idea of giving the boy the additional name of Che or Fidel for the initials, MP, with their connotation of establishment politics, were no more acceptable than MCP.

'Let's just call him something simple like Harold,' suggested Arthur. 'That at least has no political overtones or undertones and HM Prendergast is not a bad label to go through life with.'

So HM Prendergast it was and on the very same day a baby girl they called Penelope was born to Pansy Harper and Darius Deering.

It was no secret that George Hood-Phillips was a homosexual. Some of the worker members of the National Revolutionary Committee still made uneasy jokes about such matters but they were quickly learning to be ashamed of their archaic responses. What brought Hood-Phillips's revolutionary career to an end was not his homosexuality but the expression of it by his cohabitation with a Special Branch officer. Not that he knew it when they first met but by the time he did discover it, it was too late. It was not a trap; they were head over heels in love with each other. Clementina was particularly shocked when the news broke. 'Where would the movement be,' she asked rhetorically, 'if we all went around screwing cops?'

There was clearly no answer to this and both the

authorities and the NRC decided that it would be in their best interests to hush things up. Hood-Phillips, it was agreed, would take a back seat and the Special Branch officer was assigned to traffic duties where, it was felt, neither his sexual preferences nor his revolutionary connections would affect his performance.

Hood-Phillips's natural successor as a chairman of the standing sub-committee of the National Revolutionary Committee, in essence, leader of the Party, was Arthur, it being agreed that the worker members would not identify with the conscience of the Reverend Hilary Jones, and would abandon any organization run by a black man or an actress. Ben Shepherd, on the other hand, would be too coherent to inspire total confidence in the academic members of the movement.

Arthur, with Clementina at his side and the baby Harold Mao in a carrycot, between them became national and international figures. They were indefatigable in their marching and were frequently pictured in protective stances over their baby amid the stones and gas-grenades of battle. Afterwards they would go on television and answer criticisms of their action in involving the baby in brawls by declaring that it was his future and the future of millions of other babies all over the world that they were fighting to protect. Bad as the police charges were, they said, they could not be compared to what would happen when the bomb was dropped.

Harold Mao was ten years old and an expert in revolutionary street tactics when his mother, now in the full glory of her beauty, went to Sofia to play the leading role in an Anglo-Bulgarian co-production. There she fell in love with her leading man, announced that she had discovered a socialist paradise, and said that henceforward she would only return to England for brief visits to see her beloved son. Her feelings for Arthur, she confided to a woman columnist who flew out to Sofia on hearing the news, had died some years before and she had stayed with him only out of loyalty to the movement.

Arthur never discussed Clementina's action with Harold who was left more and more to his own devices, Arthur having to travel abroad frequently on revolutionary business. He was on an official visit to China when the Lee Chin Yu story broke. Lee Chin Yu – or as he was known in England, Leigh Ormerod – was the son of a Chinese woman and a Hong Kong businessman who had deserted her as soon as he found out she was pregnant. The girl had returned to China proper and the child she bore had grown up a loyal son of the revolution, a dedicated Maoist all the more fervent because he had the aspect of a foreign devil. There was, in fact, no trace of his Chinese ancestry in his face and, as he grew older, he more and more took on the appearance of the bluff Manchester businessman his father had been before moving to Hong Kong to export cotton shirts to his native country.

The Peking Intelligence Authorities, whose ambition to penetrate the British Secret Service had been thwarted for years because of ethnic factors outside their control, were quick to see the possibilities in Lee's physiognomy and trained him from an early age in English, ciphers and sabotage. They equipped him with false papers and sent him to England with orders to lead a blameless life for at least ten years before becoming active. Lee, it came out in subsequent court proceedings, had followed his instructions perfectly, spending the first four years at university where he managed to avoid attracting any attention at all by becoming chairman of the Conservative Society. He then joined the Foreign Office where he passed all security checks with ease until he found himself assistant head of the Far East Section. For the next five years he had left a weekly precis of his Section's thoughts and activities in a hollow tree in a Bloomsbury square.

He would have remained undiscovered if a number 73 bus had not careered into the tree totally demolishing it to reveal the packet of papers in Chinese script. The Special Branch, acting with commendable speed, quickly erected a dummy tree in its place and kept a round-the-clock vigil. They were eventually rewarded by the sight of the Deputy Head of the Far East Section of the Foreign Office, totally deceived by the polyurethane skill of the tree-maker, slip his weekly report into what he took to be its accustomed place.

It was while Arthur was in Peking on his fraternal visit that Leigh Ormerod, alias Lee Chin Yu, was sentenced to 42 years' imprisonment by a British judge. The Chinese Government, in retaliation, told Arthur that he must not leave his hotel room and quietly indicated to the British Government that they were willing to do a deal. The Prime Minister held a Cabinet meeting in which he plainly stated the choice that lay before them. 'We can either exchange this Chinese spy who is at least half a traitor for Arthur Prendergast, leader of the National Revolutionary Committee, or let them both rot, the Chink here and the Red there.'

He sternly rebuked the Secretary of State for Foreign Affairs who by this time was rolling on the carpet and asked him, when he was fully recovered, to draft a note pointing out to the Representative of the People's Republic of China that Her Majesty's Government had no power whatsoever over the British judicature and that if, as a regrettable result of their inability to act in this matter, Arthur Prendergast, an innocent citizen of the United Kingdom, was illegally held in his Chinese hotel room for the next 42 years, the responsibility for this inconceivably illegal act would be the Chinese Government's alone.

* * *

Arthur Prendergast in his room in Peking; Clementina in her flat in Sofia, HM, now 17, at his school in Hampshire, Pansy Harper, Darius Deering and their daughter Penny at their university town in the West of England, all decided about this time that they wanted a change of life. Pansy ran off with a guitar player and Darius, when he found her, gave her enough money to buy herself a small boarding house in a seaside resort before gratefully returning to America. Penny, given the choice, preferred to stay in England because she had decided to be an actress and everyone knew that English acting was better than American acting. With her father's help she enrolled at a university drama course just before shortage of funds caused it to be terminated. But even that small experience was helpful to her in getting a job as assistant stage manager at a Midlands repertory theatre. HM had frequently travelled to London to see Foreign Office officials about his father but his heart wasn't in it as he had had enough of both his parents by the time he was ten. His feelings for his mother still lingered on but they had been attenuated when she did not answer any of the fourteen letters he sent her in the twelve months after she had set up residence in Bulgaria. It never occurred to HM to go to university and after he left his boarding school he lived for a time in his father's flat in Hampstead. When he ran out of money, the bank manager pointing out to him gently that, as far as was known, his father was alive, HM quietly sold the contents of the flat to a shady dealer from Camden Town and moved into a room in that vicinity.

Clementina decided to abandon both Boris and Bulgaria and come home. Boris had become very possessive and the Bulgarian Secret Police had become far too noticeable. The strain had proved too much for Boris and one night he blacked both her eyes after accusing her of looking directly at the secret policeman, something that was so contrary to etiquette that it could only be construed as a sexual invitation. Clementina felt that at the age of forty she could no longer allow this kind of interference with her appearance and returned to London only to find the flat she had inhabited with Arthur empty of furniture and full of squatters.

Arthur, who wished to change his way of life more genuinely and more deeply than any of them, languished in his hotel room in Peking. He had anticipated being released after Mao's death and all the subsequent changes and, no doubt, the Chinese authorities would have relented had they been pressed by the British Government. The British Government, however, though it had changed character on a number of occasions, took the view that Arthur was probably happier where he was and made no overtures to the powers in Peking.

The world moved on in many different ways and directions. Many things changed, mostly for the worst. But that is the story so far. Now read on.

Chapter 1

Once it had been a warehouse in Covent Garden and it was still warm with the memory of ancient fruit. Oranges and lemons, apples, pears, apricots and, later, mangoes, lychees, watermelons and guavas, had all at one time or another fractured their rinds or burst their soft skins in the corners of the darkened rooms and allowed their sweet juices to seep into the grimy floorboards. Fearsome, frightened spiders, shipped from Jamaica inside crates of green bananas, had scuttled into corners to wait for prey that never came and had died there of malnutrition. Peaches and plums had rotted, their stones finding no foothold on the unyielding floor. There had once been hundreds of such storehouses, huge echoing caverns which, when cleared of their contents, still held a heady, fruit-scented air. Exotic fruits, as commonplace as the cabbages that came in convoys of juggernauts; the produce of Jersey and Guernsey and market gardens from Kent to The Fylde, things grown under glass or dug up from fields, gathered from bushes, picked from trees, spread out to dry or kept fresh with water, had provided the place with its purpose. Once they had been removed to somewhere more convenient the area had lain derelict for a while like a place exhausted by an earthquake. Then slowly, movement returned. A restaurant chanced its arm and opened; an art gallery, unaccustomed to such expansive wall space, spread its fledgling wings; shops opened selling copperware, basketware, footware, whole foods and herbs, oriental spices, second-hand bicycles, gadgets, knick-knacks and contrivances of all kinds; more galleries and restaurants followed, the pubs licked themselves clean and bright with new paint and, within a matter of months, it was a spanking, brand-new tourist attraction in which only the highest class of huckster was allowed to operate. Deterioration set in within a few years. The imperatives of greed took charge and high prices and high rents resulted in bankruptcies and the straight, old-fashioned flit. Shops and warehouse space became available once again and were either left to gather dirt and dust or plunged to the cheaper end of trade. One warehouse remained as a reminder of the old arts and crafts and little theatre days of the eighties. The painted sign above the door, lit by a grimy lamp, faintly announced that it was the Total Art Environment. Besides the doorway was a poster which read:

Break down the Barriers!
Rock Action Theatre
in
The All-Molecular-Genetic-
Catatonic Show
SCREAM!
plus a
Paranoia Presentation
ART FOR THE PEOPLE!
A multi-Media Culture Shock
Guide to the new Reality
See
The TV Eye
The Battered Baby
Living Sculptures
Kinetics
Licensed Bar

HM read the poster carefully and had just reached the words 'Licensed Bar' when he felt the brilliant flash of light almost palpably hit the side of his face. He turned round, slowly.

'Most people,' said the wild-haired, brown-skinned, large-framed, wide-smiling, bright-eyed man who stood there winding on his camera. 'Most people jump when I do that.'

HM said: 'You only took a picture.'

The man looked at his watch. 'It's time,' he said. 'Will you take one of me.' He handed his camera to HM without waiting for an answer. HM looked through the view-finder, stepped back to get the lean, stubbled face into focus and pressed the button. 'Thanks man,' said the photographer. 'It's just for the record.'

'That's all right,' said HM, politely.

'You don't mind then?'

'Mind? Why should I mind?'

'You don't want to know why?'

HM turned to go into the Total Art Environment. 'Not particularly,' he said.

'You mean you don't care what record?'

'No.'

The photographer held out his hand and HM shook it cordially. 'Nice to meet you,' the photographer said. 'You going in there?'

'Yes.'

'It's a great show. Two great shows. Which one's pulling you in man – Rock Action or Paranoia?'

'I know someone in the play,' said HM.

'You just gotta see them both,' said the photographer. 'I'm Paranoia in person. Come on in.'

On the other side of the door a girl sat at a table at the beginning of a long, dimly-lit passage lined with old posters.

'Hi Freedom,' said the girl to the photographer. She looked at HM. 'That'll be one-eighty,' she said.

The photographer said 'Hi Julie' and looked apologetically at HM as if his invitation to go on in should have had the effects of a free pass. 'Sorry about that man,' he said as HM pocketed the cloakroom ticket he had been given in exchange for his money. 'But we just gotta take some bread from someone. I'll tell you what – to make up I'll give you a personally conducted tour.'

The corridor they were in was one of a number of tunnels that radiated, like the spokes of a cartwheel, from a central hub area. Apart from the entrance tunnel itself the others either terminated at the opposite end of the hub in a bulbous performance or exhibition area or hairpinned back to the centre. It was impossible to go from one activity to another without going through the hub where the licensed bar, a table with plastic cups and a coffee machine in front of a shelf bearing a few dusty bottles was situated. Cheap wine in two litre bottles seemed to be the drink most in demand. Two bearded men and a girl sat on a bench staring silently into their plastic cups.

'We get busier when the show starts,' said HM's companion. 'It's an hour yet. Come on, I'll show you round.' He led HM into one of the tunnels. A sharp white spotlight hit a glass dome, a baby's head painted on its bald contours. Over the dome a heavy mallet was suspended by a thread. As they walked past it they triggered a switch and the light snapped off to be replaced by a glowing screen carrying the image of a naked, pregnant woman. When that faded it was replaced by an interior-lit bottle of blood-red liquid threshed into motion by the propeller of a toy sunken boat. A yard further, HM was confronted with a photograph of a naked old woman with sagging breasts. He turned and there was a screen bearing a painting with parts that spun round; a television screen flashed on, filled with a huge eye, its pupil a fragmented revolving mirror. And all the time electronic music sighed and screamed, a menagerie of sound orchestrated to signify suffering.

'Total assault,' said the photographer. 'Total assault on all the senses at once.'

HM felt a filament of some soft material cling to his face and he brushed it away. 'Let it happen man,' said the photographer. 'Let it touch you. Touch, hear, see.'

They passed a machine which belched aromatic smoke at them. 'Smell.' He took a deep breath.

'People gotta have their senses stimulated man,' he said. 'But no chemicals, no substances, no foreign bodies. Every drug we need is already there. Inside. You just gotta stir up the glands, release the fluids, tap the sources, control the emissions, turn on the juices, make the connections. So how do you do it? You stimulate the senses. All the senses, not just the five they talk about.'

He spun HM around.

'The sense of direction.'

A shot rang out.

'A sense of danger.' He looked reprovingly at HM. 'Most people jump, man,' he said. 'But,' he remembered, 'you didn't jump at the flash either.'

The music had been replaced by a loud ticking noise.

'A sense of time,' hazarded HM.

'You catch on quick, man,' said the photographer, delighted.

'A sense of humour?' HM asked.

'If you haven't got that,' said the photographer, 'you don't make it through the front door.'

'Common sense?'

'We're working on it.'

They were back at the centre of the hub which was filling up, mainly with men. HM was surprised to see that most of them were of formal appearance with reasonably short haircuts mostly wearing jeans that were both pressed and unfaded. There were even a couple of suits.

'Cops,' said the photographer. 'They check us out every night. They work a shift system.'

'It must help the box-office.'

The photographer gave him a pitying look. 'How,' he asked, 'do you charge a guy who's got a search warrant?'

He took HM up a corridor that widened out into an auditorium filled with benches and ended in an empty space which was clearly a performance area. The front bench was marked 'Reserved'. There were already a number of people sitting in the other rows. The photographer took HM to the second row from the front and asked its occupants to move up. 'You sit here,' he said. 'You'll be able to see all right. I gotta go take some pictures. After the show come up to the office for a drink. See you.'

The policemen HM had seen in the bar filed in and occupied the front row, sitting almost at attention, their arms folded or spread at the top of their thighs. They were silent. The other seats started to fill and the house lights darkened as the stage lighting came up to reveal people drifting on to the stage, moving in a seemingly haphazard somnambulistic walk until they formed two groups, one of men, one of women.

'We the oppressed!' chanted the women.

'We the oppressors!' responded the men.

'We the chained!' continued the women.

'We the forgers of chains,' proclaimed the men.

A pool of light spread on to the centre of the acting arena and Clementina stood there in a plain white blouse and black skirt. She whipped off the blouse and cupping her breasts in her hands proferred them to the audience and intoned: 'They use these for selling petrol, motor cars, music centres, deodorants.'

'Give us back our smell,' cried the women.

'For selling boots,' declaimed Clementina.

The men sank writhing to the floor, their arms outstretched in a pantomime of passion. In tones of remorse they chorused: 'They have our babies and we sell motor cars.'

The women formed a group in the spotlight while the men in pairs strutted round them, parodying male attitudes.

'There was this little dolly bird . . . there was this chick . . . hop in kid, I said, how far do you go?'

The women were derisive. 'Birds, chicks, dolls – balls!' they shouted.

The men on the bench in front of HM started to nudge each other and leaned forward in anticipation as the women ripped off their blouses and skirts.

Clementina, now stark naked, shrieked: 'We bear the children and the pain.'

The girls around her dropped to their knees and placed a large paper hoop in front of her body. A naked young man, having crawled between Clementina's legs, burst through the hoop and lay writhing on the floor howling like a baby. Now the whole company, men and women, were writhing on the floor except for Clementina who stood upright, noble, a woman martyred on the rack of biology and social conditioning. It took a few seconds for HM to realize that the screams were becoming less orchestrated, more real. Those on the stage were clutching at each other irrespective of sex, indeed, some of the girls had run to the men. A rat ran across the arena and disappeared into the gloom at the back. Then there were more rats, darting, dodging, zig-zagging among the legs. They were clearly in the audience as well. HM felt one brush past his leg and felt the bench he was sitting on vibrate as people jumped to stand on it. He was aware of the photographer who had called himself Paranoia in person standing at the end of one bench taking photographs. Then the row of policemen in front of him rose and pushed their way to the exit, clubbing anyone who stood in their way. One truncheon hit him a glancing blow and he went down. He was not unconscious for more than a few seconds but when he picked himself up both rats and people were gone and the room was empty except for two figures standing in the centre of the stage. One was Clementina, the other a young girl. They had their arms around each other. HM took off his jacket and put it around Clementina's shoulders. The three of them went through the curtains at the back of the stage and Clementina led the way up a staircase until they came to a door marked 'Freedom Wayne, Artistic Director, Total Art Environment'. They went in.

There was a clutter of peeling posters on the walls, a battered desk, a sagging sofa, a rug on the floor. The photographer was pouring whisky into a paper cup and he handed it to a woman who was shaking with either fear or indignation. On her skirt, at thigh level, was the clear imprint of a large male foot. She was covered in dust. Her body, straining against the severe cut of the black suit she wore, was made for a taller woman, a little pink hat, now tilting over her forehead, was not designed to obscure her grey hair. Clementina rushed towards the photographer.

'Oh Freedom,' she said, HM's jacket falling from her shoulders. Freedom put his arms around her. 'You were great, baby,' he said. HM picked up his jacket and put it around the shoulders of the girl who stood next to him. The woman in the suit held out her now empty cup and said, 'For God's sake Freedom give me another drink.' Freedom, pouring generously, offered an explanation. 'Dora was caught in the rush.'

'Rush,' said Dora. 'More like a bloody stampede. They fucking walked over me.'

HM said: 'They walked over me too.'

Freedom said: 'The difference is, kid, that Dora is the Minister of Culture. She's not used to being walked over, except by the Prime Minister. Isn't that true, Dora?'

'You're damned fucking right,' said Dora.

Clementina disengaged herself from Freedom's arm, raised her own dramatically and declared: 'This young man saved my life, saved us both from being eaten alive.'

'It was nothing,' said HM modestly.

Clementina ignored him and turned to Dora. 'It really is time you people did something about those bloody rats, Dora. This kind of thing just can't go on. Look what happened at the National last week – and right in the middle of the Scottish play too. Please dear – ' she held out her hand to Penny who gave her back HM's jacket. 'Thank you my sweet.'

'We're doing our best Clem dear,' said Dora. 'Every research station in the country is working on it and the Minister of Science expects a breakthrough any day now. God knows we're spending enough money on it. That's why my arts budget has been cut again.'

Clementina said: 'Freedom, do you think I could have a drink, too?'

'Sure,' said Freedom. 'You?' he asked HM.

'Yes please.'

The girl next to HM shivered and HM looked round for something to put around her shoulders. The only thing he could see was a curtain that hung over the window so he ripped it down and handed it to her.

Freedom said: 'Good thinking man' and gave the girl a cardboard cup.

'Come and sit next to me child,' said Dora, patting the sofa.

'So it was our little Penny,' said Freedom to HM.

'Penny?'

'Your friend, the one you said you had in the show.'

'I'm Penny,' said the girl on the sofa.

'No,' said HM. 'I mean we've never met. She was just standing there. Shaking.'

Clementina peered at him myopically.

'Don't I know that voice,' she said. 'My damn glasses are in the dressing room.'

'Hello mother,' said HM.

'Oh God,' said Clementina. 'It's HM, isn't it?'

'Yes mother.'

Clementina recovered her composure. 'Darling,' she cooed, embracing him, oblivious to the fact that she was wearing only a jacket. 'It's been simply ages. How are you?'

'Fine.'

'I was fine too until those damn rats arrived.' An even sharper note of irritation appeared in her voice. 'Freedom, will you please go out there and get my clothes.'

'And mine,' said Penny.

Freedom put down the bottle of whisky on his desk and moved towards the door. 'Help yourselves,' he said.

Dora was solicitous. 'You look cold, dear,' she said to Penny. 'Have another drink.' She gestured to HM to bring the bottle over and he did as he was motioned.

'Me too, HM,' said Clementina.

Penny said: 'HM?'

'Harold Mao,' said HM. 'It was her idea.'

'Not mine darling,' said Clementina. 'Your father's. I wanted to call you Fidel Ché. He was a couple of historic revolutionaries,' she explained to Penny. 'Before your time, darling. Before mine for that matter,' she hastily added.

Freedom came back into the room.

'All gone, rats, clothes, audience, cops, all gone.' He turned to Clementina. 'You'd better go up to the flat and get some more.'

'You and your damned rats!' snarled Clementina.

'Not my rats, baby,' said Freedom cheerfully. 'Government rats. Tested, officially classified, technologically perfect, grade one government issued rats.' He stressed the word 'issued'.

'You've heard then,' Dora said gloomily. 'I told the PM we'd never be able to keep it quiet.'

She looked at HM and thought that here was someone who was owed an explanation. People often felt that about HM. 'You see,' she said, 'we bred a special group of rats for research purposes – something to do with genetic engineering. There was a law about doing it with human beings. They escaped and, being superior in many ways to your average rat, they've multiplied in their millions down there. Every now and again the overcrowding gets a bit too much for them and there's a kind of mass breakout.'

'They go over the wall,' said Freedom.

'So they come up and look for a new place,' said Dora, ignoring him, 'and when they find one that's suitable they settle down and keep quiet until they get overcrowded again. The trouble with these rats is that they breed like rabbits.'

'The trouble is,' said Freedom, 'that they mixed with those rats that were already immune to every known poison and there's now no way of getting rid of them without killing everyone else in the process.'

Dora sighed. 'You heard about that too, did you? Our security is getting very slack. I just don't see the point in having an Official Secrets Act when everybody goes round telling a pack of truths. I'm sorry they ruined your play, my dear,' she said to Clementina.

'Ruined the play! Sod the play. If it hadn't been for – for my son here I would have been eaten alive. Even the fuzz in the front row panicked.'

'All the same,' said Freedom, 'it was great, the first

real thing that has happened in this place since I started it.'

'A sense of reality,' said HM.

Freedom looked startled for a moment. 'What? Yeah, that's right man, that's right. A sense of reality. You see Dora why we need this grant. We gotta make more things happen. The whole idea is too static. We have arts shows and plays and music, but none of it really touches anyone . . .' Without stopping he looked at his watch and handed his camera to Clementina who took a photograph of him, wound on the film and put the camera back on the desk. 'They come in here and grope each other in the cinema or slip into the theatre to look at Clem and the girls – or boys – but nothing really touches them. Until tonight, that is. Boy, they sure came in contact with reality tonight.'

'If you think,' said Dora indignantly, the little dyed feathers on her hat quivering, 'I am going to give you money so that you can frighten people into trampling all over me you must be mad, Freedom. I'm going home. Does anybody want a lift. My driver's outside somewhere. Where do you live, my dear,' she asked Penny.'

'I'm going upstairs to get some sleep,' said Clementina. 'You sure they've gone Freedom?'

Penny said: 'The fact is I'm not sure.'

'Sure,' said Freedom, 'they've gone.'

'You're not sure?' asked Dora betraying some surprise. 'How can you not be sure?'

'We mustn't lose touch again, darling,' said Clementina to HM. 'Come round tomorrow and I'll take you to lunch and we'll have a lovely long talk. I want to hear all about you and all the marvellous things you've been doing.'

'The fact is,' said Penny, 'I was living here until Clementina moved in a couple of days ago. So I share a place with one of the girls now. I guess she's gone and I'm not really sure I could find it by myself. Besides, those were the only clothes I had with me, the ones I left on the stage, the ones that've gone.'

'In that case,' said Dora with pleasure in her voice for the first time that evening, 'you had better come home with me.'

'Okay,' said Penny. 'Can I borrow your curtain, Freedom?'

'Sure baby.'

'There's a blanket in the car,' said Dora. 'It will be warmer and cleaner. Would you be an angel HM?'

HM found his way into the deserted street and saw the big black government limousine standing half on the pavement. It was the only vehicle in sight. There was no sign of a driver. The window on the front nearside door was open and when he put his hand inside and opened the door itself the interior light came on. The plastic upholstery was full of little rips, from claws or teeth HM couldn't tell. There was no rug on the back seat. He heard a movement and saw two beady eyes fixed on him from the gloom beneath the steering wheel. Without taking his eyes off the rat, HM opened the door wide and stepped back. The two unwavering stares, HM's and the rat's locked into each other and then the rat moved towards the open door, limping on three legs, the fourth held stiffly off the ground having probably been stamped on or kicked. By whom? The driver, thought HM. Where was he then? The rat jumped on to the pavement and, without fear, hobbled away.

HM tried to pierce the gloom under the steering wheel of the big car. His eyes were taken by something glinting. He picked up a brass button. He found a torch in the glove box and by its light found four more large buttons and two smaller ones. There was no sign of anything else.

'They must have eaten the blanket and the rest of the jacket,' said Dora firmly when HM showed her what he had found.

'What do you think happened to the driver?' asked Penny, voicing everyone else's thoughts.

'God knows,' said Dora. 'But if you are asking if he was eaten in the car I would think the answer is no. It's my guess he had left the jacket over the back of the seat and had got out of the car to stretch his legs when the rats came. He probably just ran. The rats eat any natural material.'

'But that's just guesswork, isn't it,' said Freedom. 'They could just as easily have eaten him.'

'No,' said Dora, 'HM would have found some bones. They eat everything but the bones. HM would have found bones if he had been caught in the car. Of course they could have got him when he ran but so far they have not attacked people who are awake and can kick out.'

HM remembered the rat with the broken or injured leg. He had not told them about that. But Dora was probably right; after all, he had found no bones. It stood to reason that there would be bones. What was that she was asking him?

'I said can you drive young man?'

'Yes.'

'In that case,' said Dora, 'I am exercising my prerogative as a member of the Government and ordering you to drive me home.'

'I don't mind,' said HM.

'It wouldn't matter if you did,' snapped Dora.

'That,' thought HM, 'is what you think.' But he drove her and Penny home all the same. When they reached the block of Grade 1 Security Status flats assigned to members of the government and heads of nationalized industries, Dora saw them both through the machine, computer and visual checks – in Penny's case all she had to do was draw the curtain – she took them up to her eighth and therefore top floor apartment. The high-security blocks had been built after the co-ordinated terrorist attack in the late-eighties in which fourteen guards and three junior ministers had been killed in a combined operation by Irish, Arab, Basque, Iranian, Libyan, Syrian and Iraqi forces who, at an international conference in Tripoli had decided that it was all the fault of the British Government which would be fully responsible for any bloodshed which resulted from its failure to do as they wished and had selected three comparatively unimportant members of the government for assassination as a mark of its sincerity of purpose. The security forces had wished to have fewer blocks of flats to guard but that would have meant that they would have been built higher and that would have been contrary to the legislation brought in a decade earlier after the Prendergast disaster. True, a large number of Prendergast buildings were still standing but that was because bringing them down was a costly business and only those that were on the point of collapsing were demolished. The rest, it was felt, were safe enough as long as they were not inhabited.

Dora left HM alone in the sitting room of her flat while she took Penny into the bedroom to find her some clothes. HM examined the two dralon-covered settees which faced each other over the low central radiator, inspected the banks of video-cassette books, most of them on political science and economy, a few reference works on music and drama, autobiographies of politicians and playwrights and a sprinkling of Sapphic works whose titles he recognized from the shelves of the female teachers' common room at school. There were some bottles and glasses on a side-table.

'You can pour me one too,' said Penny who had changed her curtain for a white bathrobe. 'Dora's in the kitchen making some sandwiches.'

It was only then that HM realized how hungry he was.

Dora came in with a mountain of sandwiches, poured

herself a large whisky, sat on the sofa next to Penny, put her hand on the girl's knee and sighed with content. 'It's good to be home,' she said. But it was as if even a moment's relaxation was unbearable. Somewhere the valve that controlled her political anger opened and energy coursed through the compressed curves of her body as she jumped to her feet. 'This rat thing must be stopped before we're all eaten alive – or trampled to death. It amounts to the same thing.'

She took off her shoe and hammered on the wall with it. 'He lives next door, Bendigo, the Science Minister,' she explained. There was an answering tap. 'Good, he's in. Do eat up you two, you look half-starved.'

She herself picked up two sandwiches and bit through both of them at the same time. 'It saves using the phone,' she said. 'The PM's always on to us about the size of our telephone bills. He believes most phone calls are unnecessary and all phone calls go on too long.'

The front door bell rang.

'That will be the Minister,' said Dora. 'Would you mind letting him in HM? If Penny went he would take ten minutes to get through the hall. Disgusting old groper.' She gave Penny's knee another squeeze.

Richard Bendigo, Minister of Science and Lotteries, was a short, plump, balding, good-humoured, greedy man, all appetite. He had to swallow the saliva that came into his mouth as he entered the room, though whether the cause was the sight of the sandwiches, the drink or Penny, HM was unsure.

'Greetings Dora,' said Bendigo, making straight for the sandwiches. He put two into his mouth, picked up two more, put them on one of the plates Dora had provided, moved to the side-table, poured himself a large whisky and sat down on the sofa on the other side of Penny. 'Who is this delightful girl, Dora?' he said, hastily swallowing the mouthful of sandwich so that he should not speak with his mouth full. 'Your taste is improving. Or does she belong to the young man who so kindly let me in?'

'She belongs to no one Richard,' said Dora disapprovingly. 'Not as far as I know, anyway. The only reason they are both here is that your damned rats devoured Alfred – '

'Alfred?' asked Bendigo.

'My driver,' said Dora continuing without pause, 'broke up a dramatic performance in which Penny here was appearing and resulted in my nearly being trampled to death by some young hooligans who, it was explained to me later, were members of our wonderful or mainly wonderful, that is, with a few rare exceptions not at all characteristic of the general mass, police force. At least they *could* have eaten Alfred. The one thing for sure is that he has disappeared and left only his brass buttons behind him. I have already warned Penny about your gross habits, Richard.'

'Take no notice of her, my dear,' Bendigo said cheerfully, patting Penny's other knee. 'She does not understand these matters. No head for science either. If you had, Dora, you'd understand that everything possible is being done. I shall have something to tell the House very shortly.'

'Don't give me that crap,' said Dora sharply. 'The truth is you haven't the faintest idea of how to deal with the problem.'

Bendigo laughed. 'The Government is full of ministers who haven't the slightest idea of how to deal with the problems they are supposed to be solving. Or if they have an idea some other minister tells them it is not possible. I am a Minister like you, Dora. You cannot act, write or compose music, yet you are responsible, as Minister of Culture, for seeing that all these activities flourish. You are also responsible as Minister for Coal-mining for negotiating terms to end the annual strike. Yet you yourself have never mined coal – or, for that matter, ever been on strike, despite all your radical talk. You do all these things by trusting those you are supposed to have confidence in – '

' – and sacking them if they don't come up with the right answer,' snapped Dora.

'Exactly,' said Bendigo, 'and I expect I can match you man for man – sorry, person for person – in the number of sackings we've both achieved. If only our effectiveness could be judged on that. Is it one or two you have demoted in the eighteen months we've been in office, Dora? But the civil servants are not the same as the technicians or, in this case, the scientists. I've got the best team of scientists in Britain working on the rat problem. They get every penny they need and every facility they ask for. What more can I do? What more can even my senior civil servants do? I'm Minister of Science and Public Lotteries, not a bloody scientist or a statistician. The thing is these bloody rats are not only resistant to everything we put down but actually seem to thrive on the stuff.'

He leaned forward, eager to explain and shift fractionally closer to Penny. He had obviously been well-briefed. 'The old poisons worked by causing uncontrollable bleeding from any minor rupture of the blood vessels. After four or five days the rat died. It was messy and painful, but most people detest rats and happily accepted a solution which they would not tolerate for other vermin such as the grey squirrel, the fox or the wood pigeon. There was also the additional factor that the rats had the decency to express their anguish in the privacy of the sewers. There was another poison, a narcotic which lowered the body temperature to the point where the rat actually died from exposure as if he had been lying on an open raft in the Northern Approaches for twenty-four hours in mid-winter. Today's rats are immune to both methods – and immune also to the other seventy-five poisons we experimented with last year. Even the highly dangerous ones like zinc phosphate.'

'But if you don't come up with something soon,' said Dora, 'we'll be fighting them for the food we put in our mouths.'

Bendigo, his mouth full after taking another bite on his sandwiches, said: 'We are already. We were working on a scheme to convert the old North Sea oil rig platforms into grain storage tanks. The grain would be pumped through the pipe lines as and when it was wanted.'

'That sounds like a bright idea,' said HM.

'What went wrong?' asked Penny.

'Naturally,' said Bendigo, 'the scheme was an official secret. Equally, everyone knew about it except a genius by the name of Inskip on a remote research station near Slough. He decided to introduce a lemming strain into rats in the belief that they would all swim out to sea and commit mass suicide whenever overcrowding reached an intolerable level. It was a fairly simple matter to isolate the swimming gene and implant it into a couple of rats. The result is that we quickly created a breed of rat which is a strong swimmer but, unfortunately, not the least bit suicidal. As quickly as we converted the oil platforms to grain storage bases the bloody rats swam out to them. They even got into the pipe lines. We had to abandon the idea.'

'If we don't do something soon,' said Dora, 'it could bring us down. I said as much to the PM the other day. By the way Richard, have you noticed something odd about the PM? I could have sworn – '

'Pas devant, Dora, pas devant. Sorry children,' Bendigo said apologetically to HM and Penny, 'but anything appertaining to the PM is covered by the Official Secrets

Act. Technically, I believe, it is an offence to disclose who the Prime Minister actually is. But it leaked out quite early on and doesn't seem to have done any harm.'

'There's talk in the circles in which I move,' said Dora, 'of taking to the streets again. It's all talk of course. It would be quite impossible now. But it indicates the depth of feeling these rats have aroused.'

'Demos!' said Bendigo, his face lighting up. 'Those were the days, eh, Dora? When we stood side by side and marched for our ideals. Against racism, against nuclear war, against unemployment, against – oh against everything. We made our voices heard in the land, eh? By God we did. If they start the demos again I've a good mind to join 'em. They made you feel so – alive.'

'Rubbish,' said Dora. 'I remember my grandfather talking about World War Two like that, Richard, and for very much the same reason. You were young. A fine fool you'd look now waving a banner demanding the sacking of the Science Minister. Anyway, there hasn't been a proper demo for years. There couldn't be, could there?'

Bendigo was sad. 'I never really approved of the immobilization gases,' he said. 'Physically harmless they may have been but they sapped the spirit, particularly the spirit of protest.'

'Things were getting out of hand,' said Dora. 'I didn't mind fighting the police or the fascists or the Right in general. But when they started going for us, for our own people, it was the bloody limit. Dammit, we were the only ones trying to help them. I remember one brute, all of six foot he was, I had to hit him over the head with a bottle to stop him from half-killing me.'

'Come off it Dora,' said Bendigo. 'How could you reach?'

'We were both lying down in the road at the time,' said Dora as if she was explaining something obvious to a half-wit. 'He was on top of me and there happened to be a spare bottle nearby.'

'Maybe he wasn't attacking you but making love to you,' suggested Bendigo.

'It amounts to the same thing,' said Dora. 'And he got the same response. No, something had to be done.'

'Maybe,' said Bendigo gloomily. 'But I'm not convinced that the IGs didn't do more harm than good in the long run. What we need every now and again is a good old-fashioned outburst of public anger. It's not important whether it's justified or not; it's not even important whether it's directed at the right people or not. What is important is that it is seen to be there. People don't seem to get angry any more.'

'That's why we need culture,' said Dora. 'Or at least the theatre. That way they can go and see other people being angry – or pretending to be angry which amounts to the same thing if the acting's good enough. It does them good, gives them an outlet, allows them to let off – '

'Apathy,' interrupted Bendigo. 'That's what they let off, apathy.'

'A lot of what you say is right,' said Dora. 'But it just wouldn't do to have the demos and marches start all over again. Not until we've got things more settled.'

.'I quite liked them,' said HM.

'They never achieved all that much, even when they were at their most vicious,' continued Dora.

'I'm surprised you remember them at all,' said Bendigo to HM. 'Surely you weren't really old enough?'

'Not the demos,' said HM. 'I mean I didn't like the demos. Not all that much. They were pretty boring actually. Every weekend, year in, year out, never mind the weather, marching along with mother holding my hand and shouting things like, "Power to the People!" '

'And "End the tyranny of the ballot box",' remembered Bendigo enthusiastically.

'Oh shut up Richard,' said Dora. 'So what was it you liked then?' she asked HM.

'Liked? Oh those gases you were talking about, the IGs. That was the nice bit. I was about seven or eight when they were first used. Mind you, I'd gone through all the previous experiments – I must have got my first whiff of anti-demo gas when I was still in my carrycot. I didn't like them at all.'

'They were awful,' said Bendigo. 'They made you sick as a dog,' he explained to Penny.

'They didn't make me sick,' said HM. 'It was worse than that. They made everyone else sick. And being in a carrycot when that happens is no joke. Everyone would vomit and fall down all over the place. But once the IGs came in it was great fun. Everyone suddenly rooted to the spot like that, only their eyes flickering. You could do all sorts of things to them, kid things, you know.'

'Like what?' asked Penny.

HM was uneasy. 'I was only seven or eight at the time,' he said lamely.

'Like what?' insisted Penny.

'I used to look up the girls' dresses,' said HM.

'Filthy little beast,' said Dora at exactly the same moment that Bendigo, smiling, said 'precocious boy.'

'It was only once or twice,' said HM apologetically.

'Of course it was,' said Dora. 'Once we knew we were helpless we stopped. There was no point in going on. You felt such a fool standing there for three hours or more. Sometimes in the pissing rain. Now I remember, there were always one or two kids like you, little bleeders. I suppose the stuff didn't get down there where the little perishers were.'

'It was heavier than air,' said Bendigo, thoughtfully.

‘That’s why they had to explode it over the heads of the marchers. It dropped down on them, don’t you remember, Dora? Like the gentle rain of heaven upon the mob beneath.’

‘You just stood there like a bloody statue and when the air was clear they’d all walk past and poke you with their fingers. Until the police put protective guards on us there were all sorts of little horrors like you poking at the private parts and making disgusting personal remarks. It would have been better if the stuff had blacked out the brain but it didn’t. You just stood there thinking what a bloody fool you were for three hours. Most people couldn’t stand it, though the transcendental meditators would pay anything for a small canister of the stuff. You couldn’t even make much of a fuss about the inhumanity of it; it had no after-effects.’

‘So that was it,’ said Bendigo to HM. ‘You recovered sooner for some reason or other and then got up to your revolting little tricks.’

HM laughed. ‘No. I was never affected. Don’t forget, I was taken on my first demo when I was six weeks old – ’

‘He’s Clementina’s son,’ said Dora to Bendigo. Bendigo nodded as if that explained everything.

‘ – I was at exhaust level most of the time,’ continued HM, ‘so I must have breathed more carbon monoxide than oxygen for the first eighteen months of my life. Then, like you said, I got a whiff of every single one of the riot control gases. Some were quite nice. I remember being taken to the seaside as a kid – it was a protest sit-in against some East Coast nuclear installation – and I felt quite sick until the wind changed and started blowing from the land. By the time the IGs came round, I suppose I was immune.’

‘You mean,’ said Bendigo, giving the impression that he was choosing his words very carefully, ‘you mean you built up a resistance.’

'I suppose so,' said HM, cheerfully. 'Just like your rats. It's natural isn't it? I don't see what's so surprising. It's survival by adaptation to a changing environment. Even the post-Darwinians acknowledged that it happened all the time.'

'Dora,' said Bendigo, 'this young man is going to be very important to us – '

' – I'm no scientist, Mr Bendigo,' said HM hastily. 'I was never any good at it at school. Nor at anything else, for that matter,' he added gloomily.

'Maybe not,' said Bendigo. 'But all the same I think you may have the answer to the nation's most pressing problem. You, my dear boy, are going to become famous.'

'I am?' said HM doubtfully.

'You are,' said the Minister. 'You are the new man. Don't you see – natural selection has taken you in its grasp and evolution has triumphed once again. The poisonous environment has produced the poison-resistant man. People think we've improved the atmosphere we breathe simply because we've cleared away the smoke; what the eye doesn't see the lungs don't breathe. But we have more sulphur dioxide in the London air than almost anywhere else in Europe and the fumes from our factories are killing fish in Swedish lakes and cutting a swathe through the plant life from here to Moscow. We're under constant pressure from those governments to the East of us to clean up our air and if the Atlantic were not so broad we'd be urging the Americans to do something about theirs. But it would be so costly that it would close down the few factories we've got left.'

Bendigo felt the urge for oratory coming over him as it usually did at moments of tension or excitement.

'Our day is over Dora,' he declared. 'We are finished. In this pale and weedy youngster sitting here half-pissed on your whisky is the seed of the super-race that will supersede us.'

Dora was not impressed. 'The PM has always said Richard that your greatest weakness, even at Cabinet meetings, was your inability to resist a pun.'

'The PM has many times enlarged on your weaknesses, too, Dora. They seem to exercise a more than usual fascination for him. Actually, I intended no pun. But don't you see, this was inevitable. If the rats could find a way, could mankind be so far behind? After all, we have shown ourselves to be nearly as intelligent and far more ruthless in the pursuit of survival than they have been.'

'I still don't see,' said Dora, 'what use this young man could be to you and your scientists. Unless they are going to experiment on him until they find a fatal gas. But they could do that with the rats without his help.'

Bendigo put on the special voice he usually used when explaining a complex matter to one of his dimmer constituents or a Cabinet colleague. 'We have always had two choices,' he said, taking them through his argument step by easy step. 'We could have let natural selection – evolution – take its course and wipe out those who were weak or unable to cope with the changing environment – whether we changed it or it changed of its own accord is immaterial – or we could take special measures to protect those who, for one reason or another, had less chance of survival.

'Because we did not like the way things were arranged, because we were more compassionate than evolution – or, for that matter, God – and didn't like the sight of people starving to death either because there were no natural resources or because they could not come to terms with the complex machinery of the society we had developed, we took special measures to protect the weak. When their crops failed we sent them food and when they – and our own – people could not acquire the skills that were demanded by a changing world or there was simply nothing for them to do even if they could, we gave them money and shelter and thus prolonged their lives. Don't misunderstand me; I do not say we were wrong to do this, in fact I am sure we were right. But the effect of all this compassion was that the weak survived and bred so successfully that the previously strong found it hard to adapt to the new environment that was thus created. We called it social engineering and that is precisely what it was. One part of the machine was strengthened, but only at the expense of another part. Evolution, however, does not care who goes to the wall as long as someone goes. It abhors a state of balance because that means things are static and that way there is no movement at all, just stagnation.

'The root cause of most of our problems in the 20th century was simply that people could not change quickly enough to keep abreast of conditions; whether those conditions were an improvement or a deterioration in comparison with previous environments is immaterial. Some people showed enormous powers of adaptation. Children acquired skills that their parents did not even know existed. It was not just a question of learning how to do something; there was, occasionally, and with some people, a quantum leap forward. Remember the Rubik Cube, that puzzle with several million problems and only one solution? Intelligent adults could work on it for months without finding the answer; some children did it in less than a minute. Nobody had taught them; they hadn't learned how to do it; they just knew. They had acquired a skill that no one knew existed before. If the ability to solve the Rubik Cube had automatically been accompanied by success in other areas those children, in more primitive times, would have prospered more than others and would have been more successful in rearing families who would have tended to inter-marry and so pass on their characteristics to succeeding generations. But in the age of compassion and charity that particular talent conferred on its possessor no special advantage in the way of survival. Those who did not know a cube from a cone, who didn't know Rubik from pubic, also flourished and, as the talent had no survival value, it was dispersed through the general population and eventually forgotten. It probably had no genetic foundation anyway but was an aspect of intelligence that had always been there – and still is – but which is not normally tapped simply because it is not normally required.

'No, what we need is an evolutionary change in the population of this country that could apply to everyone and advance us – or at least future generations – to a stage that would create as big a distance between us and them as there is between us and our broad-nostrilled, bone-headed ancestors. They had plenty of time; for us, time is running out; we need to enhance our ability to survive or we won't.'

Bendigo wiped the sweat off his glistening forehead and gave a nervous laugh, as if he were somehow ashamed at some of the things he had said, as if he, devoutly orthodox, had surprised himself in the act of uttering a heresy.

His voice lost its messianic note and began to plead. 'Just imagine we had the power to isolate the special factor that is at the root of evolutionary change and that we could speed up the whole process. I'm not suggesting that we create a society in which only the elite survive. We want something to benefit everyone. But we don't have the time to wait for evolution. God's greatest error was to arrange things according to his time scale and not ours. A thousand ages in his sight sees us all dead and done for.'

He remembered how it had all started and became

excited again. 'But with this stripling here, this boy who looks perfectly normal – '

'I am perfectly normal,' burst in HM indignantly.

'Normal is never perfect,' observed Dora.

Penny said nothing.

' . . . perfectly normal,' repeated Bendigo, giving no other sign that he had heard HM, 'the scientists will have something to work on – the perfect human example of the process of self-immunization, an evolutionary leap forward. All the latest theories postulate such a possibility. After all, it could only be a matter of time before a human being achieved what the rats achieved years ago. Nobody taught them how to change their genes, but change them they did. Of course, it all hangs on if what he says is true. If not – ' he shrugged and left the sentence hanging.

'If not what?' asked HM.

Bendigo laughed. 'If not we'll continue to exercise charity and put it down to a vivid imagination.'

'I don't imagine things like that,' said HM. 'There'd be no point.'

'So far Professor Redhill and his team have had only the rats to work on,' said Bendigo. 'Think of the incalculable advantages of having a co-operative human being. The professor will be wild with delight. It is an evolutionary triumph comparable with the moment that man first stood upright. First the insects became immune to the insecticides, then the pests to the pesticides. Now at last man has triumphed over the homicides.'

'Oh shut up Richard,' said Dora.

'If you think . . .' said HM at the same time and then stopped politely allowing Dora to finish.

She said: 'Haven't you got it wrong? Aren't the scientists supposed to experiment on rats for the sake of humanity, not the other way round.'

'If you think, Mr Bendigo . . .' began HM.

'But it is the other way round,' said Bendigo, ignoring him. 'Think of the country, think of humanity, the huddled masses, the wretched, the distressed . . .'

'You sound just like my mother,' said HM. 'Just because somehow I can breathe polluted air it doesn't follow that I'd survive a scientific experiment. Nothing else does. I'm not going to be shoved into a test tube – or have a test tube shoved into me for that matter. It amounts to much the same thing.'

'They would do nothing to put you at risk, to expose you to the slightest discomfort,' said Bendigo. 'You're far too precious. You'd live like a lord, or at any rate, like a pop star. And it would last longer too. I expect they would want to keep you for at least a year. When you see the way some of the laboratory rats are treated – I tell you HM, you'd be more comfortable than you've ever been in the whole of your life.'

'You'd better find some other guinea pig,' said HM. 'Even a real guinea pig. I'm tired and I want to go home.'

'I forbid you to leave these premises,' said Bendigo.

'Don't talk rubbish Richard,' said Dora. 'Take no notice of him HM. He has absolutely no authority to detain you. Where do you live?'

'Live?' said HM. Something warned him not to give his full address. 'I've got a small room in West Hampstead.'

'And how do you propose to get there tonight?' asked Dora, putting on the sensible voice that she usually reserved for elections or television interviews. 'There's no public transport, my driver has been eaten or at least has disappeared after discarding his brass buttons, all the taxi drivers go home during rat raids and if you walk you could either run into the rats or, worse still, one of the villain packs. And you're not immune from either. No, you'd better stay here. And you Penny. You can sleep on the couch HM and Penny can share with me. You don't mind Penny, do you?'

'No,' said Penny, 'I don't mind.'

'That's settled then,' said Dora. 'Richard, it's time for you to go home. We've all had a long and exciting day and I'm ready for bed.'

Bendigo said, 'But . . .'

'No buts,' said Dora. 'HM is a free citizen in a free country and if he doesn't want to be experimented on he doesn't have to be. You'll just have to get your Professor Redman – '

'Hill,' said Bendigo. 'Redhill. Though he doesn't sound like a Surrey chap I must say.'

'Redhill then,' said Dora briskly. 'You'll simply have to get him to work harder. Now good night Richard.'

She ushered him to the door and he left, a plump, glistening little visionary who turned as he was leaving the room and devoured both HM and Penny with his eyes. 'Good night then,' he said, adding, 'I'm sure we'll meet again – soon.' It wasn't clear whether he meant HM, Penny or both, but he turned and Dora patted him on the rump and steered him into the hall. They heard the door close.

A few seconds later Dora returned with a duvet which she threw at HM. 'That'll keep you warm,' she said, motioning to the sofa. 'Come on Penny.'

HM had no idea what time it was when he woke, his heart pounding, to see a dim shape standing over him. 'Ssh,' said Penny, putting her hand to his mouth. 'Dora's fast asleep, don't wake her. I think they're coming to get you in the morning.'

She sat down on the side of the bed.

'Coming? Who's coming?'

'Bendigo telephoned. We were in bed. I pretended to be asleep but I think Dora knew I was listening. She said she wouldn't have anything to do with it. I think he threatened to report her to the Prime Minister for obstruction or something if she didn't co-operate. She told him to go to hell, that she wasn't going to let him pick you up in her flat.'

'Who?' asked HM. 'Who's going to pick me up? Or not?'

'The police I suppose.'

'But I haven't done anything.'

'I don't think that matters an awful lot.'

'But if she's not going to let them . . .'

Penny's whisper became more urgent. 'Don't be so fucking innocent,' she said unexpectedly. 'Dora kept saying she wouldn't let them pick you up in her flat. Not in her flat. Outside is another matter. She even said she'd be making breakfast for you and that you'd probably leave about nine o'clock. They'll be waiting for you HM. You'll walk straight into them.'

'In that case,' said HM, sliding out from beneath the duvet, 'I'd better take my chance with the rats and the villains.'

He felt a cool hand push him back. 'There's no hurry,' said Penny. 'You can wait till it starts getting light. The streets will be clear by then.'

'If I fall asleep I'll never wake up in time,' said HM. 'I'm not used to a lot of whisky.'

'I'll stay with you,' said Penny, and she slid under the duvet beside him. Her hand slid between his legs and gently curled around his erection. 'That's better,' she said, 'much better.'

'I thought,' said HM, 'that you preferred women.'

'Dora?' said Penny, surprise in her voice. 'No, not really. I mean, she's nice and I don't mind. She needed me and now I need you. I prefer it with men physically, but emotionally – there can't be any difference can there?'

'You can't go to bed with everybody who needs you,' said HM. 'Or wants you. It amounts to the same thing. Even the fat little minister?'

'Only with people you like,' said Penny converting the

conversation into generalizations. 'The nice ones. The others, the ones who aren't nice, they have each other.'

Later, HM said: 'If I go back to my room in the morning they'll find me.'

'Go and see Freedom and your mother,' said Penny. 'They'll know what to do. I'll come with you. I can wear some of Dora's clothes. I think we'd better go; it's getting light.'

Chapter 2

To do her credit, when Dora woke up, felt for Penny and found she was not there, when she tottered into the sitting room and saw the duvet on the floor, when she opened the cupboard that served her as a wardrobe and realized that a pair of jeans, a shirt and a short denim jacket, the outfit she usually wore for cruising, were missing, she was not at all upset. She found she was remembering Penny with gratitude and HM with affection. He would, of course, be caught eventually, but at least it would be none of her doing. Bendigo would be furious. She ate a hearty breakfast.

Bendigo was furious. 'You said you'd keep him here till nine at least,' he shouted.

'I did nothing of the sort,' said Dora. 'I merely said that I would give him breakfast and that I expected he would leave about nine.'

'He must have left about five-thirty,' said Bendigo. 'I had my men here at six, as soon as it was reasonably light. They wouldn't come in the dark. I gave them strict orders to wait outside until he came out and they've been sitting there for more than three hours, the idiots.'

'You surely didn't expect them to come bursting in on me,' said Dora. 'As if I were some sort of illegal brothel, full of under-age children.'

'I don't suppose they'd dare even if you were,' said Bendigo, subsiding gloomily on to a chair and pouring himself some coffee.

'They'll soon pick him up,' said Dora cheerfully. 'He's got nowhere to go has he? Central records will already have disgorged his address. He could be silly enough to go to his mother, of course,' she mused, 'but she believes the state has a call on all its citizens so she'd probably inform on him.'

'Not this state, surely,' said Bendigo. 'Not as it is constituted now. Some noble future state perhaps. Anyway, mother-love will prevail.'

'Bollocks,' said Dora. 'Mother preservation will prevail. She's due to start a film soon, an Anglo-Albanian co-production. She won't want anything to interfere with that. She's not in such demand nowadays. She might try to take him with her, though.'

'She'd better not,' said Bendigo. 'The last thing we want is HM falling into the wrong hands. Surely even Clementina wouldn't want that, not for her worst enemy, much less her son. Can you imagine Albanian genetic engineering? God alone knows what they would produce. Not that God has even heard of Albania any more than Albania has heard of God. Why can't Clementina make films here, in England? You know, Dora, I used to adore that woman. She was the most beautiful creature. Too tall for me, of course, but I would have given anything for her, done anything. And what an actress! Her Beatrice made the heart leap.'

'Yes,' said Dora, 'I was in love with her too.'

'Did you . . . ?'

'No. We used to sit up half the night arguing politics. But she was only interested in men. Mind you, she put them through a political quiz before she would go to bed with them. You know, how do you feel about the means of production, distribution and exchange? You agree that they should be controlled by the masses? Right, take your shirt off. The abolition of Parliament? Remove your pants. A system of local Soviets? Take off my clothes. Up the workers? Right on.

'I'm not sure that she's so choosy now. Freedom isn't really a believer.'

'I was,' said Bendigo, 'that was the problem.'

'Nonsense, you would never have paid the price.'

'I would have done anything for her.'

'I don't mean that. Of course you would have lied to get into her bed, but you couldn't have followed her politically more than a yard or two down her particular road, surely to God. That's what I mean by not paying the price.'

'Social change always demands a price,' said Bendigo.

'I can't see you shooting people or locking them up – oh I don't know, that's what you want to do to HM isn't it?'

'Only for the benefit of everyone – and in the most comfortable conditions. He won't want for a thing. But I'm not keen on shooting people. Nor is Clementina come to that; her ideals wouldn't let her.'

'Don't you believe it,' said Dora. 'Cynics don't kill; it's your idealist who slaughters anyone who gets in his way. Alexander, Cromwell, Robespierre, Napoleon, Hitler, Stalin – every last one of them idealists of some sort or another. What Clementina has never come to grips with is the fact that a very large number of people would simply reject her ideals and she would have to start shooting them in order to make them see sense. God knows, the country's boring enough the way we run things, but give Clementina and her friends their way and it would be like being condemned to attend a lifelong union meeting without even the consolation of calling a strike or passing a bloody-minded resolution. And what's more, the rats, the villains and the derelict high rises would still be here.'

'I don't know, Dora,' said Bendigo, 'maybe they would be more efficient. As a Government we're not what you would call an outstanding success. Too many things go wrong.'

'Things have gone wrong with every government that's

ever had to run this country – or any other,' said Dora. 'Our record is no worse than anybody else's . . . Not much better perhaps, but no worse. If only we could get this rat business solved. And that's your pigeon Richard.'

'Well you've not been exactly helpful. It was you who let slip the most promising development in that field for years.' He sunk his head in his hands. 'Maybe,' he sighed, 'I'm the one who's inefficient. My God, it's depressing sometimes.'

'Nonsense Richard,' said Dora trying to brisk him out of his mood. 'You're a very good minister. You've got your faults of course, but on the whole you get things done. At least you've got energy. If only you didn't spend so much of it trying to get yourself into bed with some woman or other. But then, you're not the only one and I expect you'll grow out of it in time.'

'Of course I'm not the only one,' muttered Bendigo, looking hurt. 'There's you as well for a start. But as for growing out of it I only wish you were right. The trouble is I have the soul of a Casanova and the body of a butterball. If I had twice the success at sex I wouldn't need to spend half the time I do thinking about it. I suppose the really successful ones never think of it at all; they'd be too busy doing it. But you're wrong about growing out of it. I can't see any time in the future when things will be much different. You see, Dora, I like women, like being with them, touching them – even you – '

Dora said, 'Oh' but whether it was out of surprise or annoyance, Bendigo found it difficult to tell.

'And I know your tastes lie elsewhere,' he hastened to add. 'So what's there to look forward to? I'll get older and fatter and eventually impotent I suppose. But I'd have to be blind and intactile – if there is such a word – and even then they would be in my head and that's the most potent place of all.

'I sometimes sit at my desk and instead of rats and the nuclear fission problem and all the other things that should be occupying my mind, all I can see is a never-ending procession of the women I have known or met or even those I've just glimpsed in the street. Elegant women with skins like silk, Betjeman girls playing tennis and sweating in whites still warm from the airing cupboard at the top of the stairs; wild-haired girls smelling of patchouli and the doss-houses of social protest, office girls in Marks and Spencer blouses dreaming of a waiter in Benidorm, older women with faces furrowed from the men they have known – I tell you Dora the line would stretch from here to eternity, like Banquo looking at his descendent kings.'

'I know you couldn't keep your eyes off Penny last night. Or your hands whenever you got close enough. I suppose she's part of your desk-dreams now.'

'And yours too, I imagine.'

'And mine too,' acknowledged Dora. 'We spent a couple of pleasant hours together last night but I have no illusions. It was the young man she was interested in and when she thought I was asleep she went to him. I wonder where they are now.'

Chapter 3

'What we must do,' said Freedom, 'is to mobilize the media.' He stood up and struck an attitude, sketching out slogans with his fingers as if he were writing them on a wall. 'Hands off humanity!' he cried. 'No human guinea pigs!' 'Let the rats do their own dirty work!'

He sat down, satisfied with his contribution to the cause and then remembered something. He passed his camera to HM, stood up, adopted the same attitude as before, silently mouthed 'No human guinea pigs!' and looked expectantly at HM until the camera was pointed at him and the flash indicated that the shutter had been activated.

HM considered the plan of action that had been set out before him. 'On the whole,' he said, 'I'd rather have some place to hide for the time being.'

He and Penny had arrived at the Total Art Centre which, if anything, looked worse in the early morning sunlight than it had the night before. Old posters festered greyly on its walls and ancient paint-sprayed graffiti expressed uninventive obscenities, fading and inarticulate mumbles of rage from the youth of twenty years ago who were now approaching a gap-toothed middle-age and still relying on the same expletives to de-stress their aching minds. Inside, the grimy plastic-tiled corridors seemed much shorter than they had appeared to be the night before and HM noticed that there was a thick layer of dust on the glass dome that formed the baby's head over which the hammer was still suspended. There was no music and the electric motors which activated some of the exhibits had been switched off. Penny had led him past Freedom's office and, without knocking, into a bedroom where HM could dimly discern two shapes under the covers of the large bed that occupied the centre of the floor. The air was stale and Penny parted the threadbare curtains and opened a window which protested sharply. Freedom sat up, startled.

'What the fuck's the time?' he asked in a panic as if he needed to know before he could voice a justified protest at the intrusion.

'It's seven o'clock,' said Penny, 'and we need help.'

'In the morning?' asked Freedom.

'Yes, in the morning,' said Penny. 'A.M.'

Freedom groaned and dived back under the duvet.

'Come on Freedom,' said Penny. 'We need help. From you and Clem. Get up – both of you.' Her tone was sharp.

The shape beside Freedom stirred and Clementina's blonde head emerged, her face still pressed into the pillow. She said something that HM could not make out.

'We'll be down in a few minutes,' said Freedom. 'Just get the fuck out of here. Go and put some coffee on.'

Both Freedom and Clementina had strong powers of recuperation and after they had washed, dressed and drunk a mug of strong black coffee each they were ready to be indignant, especially Clementina who lived on righteous indignation as others live on adrenalin.

'Hide?' she said. 'Hide! That's not the answer darling. You've done nothing wrong. What would you be hiding from?'

Freedom said: 'What do you mean he's done nothin' wrong. You're always saying the jails are full of people who've done nothin' wrong.'

'That's not the point,' snapped Clementina. 'Let the truth be known. Trust the people.'

'That's right,' said Freedom who never saw any point in repeating himself. 'Let it all hang out.'

'Blazon it in the capitalist press,' declared Clementina.

'But,' said Freedom, 'the capitalist press is a lackey of the authorities and never prints the truth.'

Clementina looked at him pityingly. 'The truth will always prevail my darling,' she said. 'Even in a corrupt society.'

'But mother – ' started HM.

'Don't you but mother me,' she snapped. Then she sighed, forgivingly. 'Can't you bring yourself to call me Clementina or even Clem,' she asked. 'It's so much – nicer.' She was almost wheedling and it upset HM.

'It shouldn't be difficult,' he said, surprised at the tone he himself detected in his voice. 'It's not as if I've got into the habit of saying mother.'

Clementina's mouth thinned as if her teeth had scraped metal. For a moment she even looked ugly. 'If that's meant as a reproach,' she snapped, 'you can go and – '

'Don't get sidetracked Clem,' interrupted Freedom. 'We have to help this boy.'

Clementina ignored him. 'You've been very lucky,' she told HM. 'You don't know how lucky you have been. As a baby you were given a great deal of love by many different people. This taught you that love transcends nationality, race, colour or creed. As an adolescent you have been largely left to your own devices. This taught you how to fend for yourself and to reach your own conclusions about life without any pressure from the adult world. You have had all the advantages of orphanism,' she concluded, 'without any of the usual hardships. You have nothing to grumble about and you have no reason to reproach me. There's many a boy who would envy your position.'

'Heading straight for the test tube,' said HM, who did not want to argue but thought that his mother had, on the whole, over-stressed the benefits of his peculiar upbringing and had failed altogether to acknowledge its drawbacks.

He knew he was wrong but sometimes, on those rare occasions when a school friend had allowed him a glimpse of the horrors of suburban middle-class life with its stifling protectiveness, its lack of commitment, its selfishness, its insularity and, above all, its sickening tolerance, he had felt the sticky attraction of its unhealthy values. But he had always resisted the temptation to reject his mother's ideology and anyway he hadn't the faintest idea how to go about buying a house. He knew it had something to do with a mortgage and that was a word that had never been uttered in his hearing except in a tone of withering contempt.

'HM's right,' said Freedom. 'We must be practical; help him.'

Clementina, though, was into a speech. 'It is a total disgrace,' she declared, 'that those fascist pigs should try to exploit HM's great talent – '

'Talent? What talent?' HM muttered, but Clementina was not to be deterred.

' – How much longer,' she went on, passionately, 'will we tolerate these assaults on the dignity of the human race. We must rise up in our millions, we the poor, the downtrodden, the oppressed, the exploited of all races – Talent you ask – ?'

So she had heard him after all, thought HM. 'Talent? Why my darling, your talent for survival, your great, unique, Marxist talent of adaptation to a changed environment. It is exactly as Marx predicted. People will change if society changes. Human nature is not immutable. We are capable of progress. Don't you see Harold – ' it was the first time HM ever remembered his mother using his first name – 'you are an evolutionary hero.'

Carried away, Freedom jumped up and clasped HM

around the waist, picking him effortlessly off the ground and setting him up on a chair.

'Hero of the evolution,' he cried. 'Super-duper-man.' Then he handed his camera to Clementina and posed with HM while she took a picture of them both.

HM stepped down from the chair where he had been deposited.

'The point is,' he said, 'how can you help me?'

'Roger,' said Clementina, triumphantly.

'Roger who?' asked HM.

'Roger Fawcett of course,' said Freedom. 'Unjolly Roger; you must know Roger Fawcett. "Privateer." The great thing is they haven't got a bourgeois obsession with checking facts. But hang on a tick, I'm out of film and flash.'

'Why does he keep on taking pictures?' asked HM when Freedom was out of the room.

'Poor Freedom,' said Clementina. 'He's a genuine artist in every possible way except for one thing – he has no discernible talent. He can't paint, he can't write, he can't play – not even a guitar – and he can't sing.'

Penny added: 'He hasn't even got a sense of rhythm.'

'But,' went on Clementina, 'he has all the artist's need to express himself. So he hit on the idea of leaving a complete pictorial record of his life from birth to death. Even that idea hung on the fact that his father had taken a photograph of him emerging from the womb. He carries a card saying that the moment he dies a picture should be taken of his corpse. He's even left his heart and kidneys for transplant on condition that a full photographic record is kept of them being taken out of him and put into someone else. In between time he takes pictures of everything he sees and gets other people to photograph him every hour, no matter what he's doing. Sometimes it can be very disruptive. It's also very expensive but he gets a grant from a university in Nebraska or some such place and they will eventually get the collection. God knows what they'll do with it. They're going to get some pretty weird pictures.'

Penny said: 'The trouble is that he's not really got much of a talent for photography either. A lot of the pictures are out of focus. But he's working on it.'

'Where does he come from?' asked HM. 'Is he American?'

'No,' said Clementina. 'He only talks like that. He was born here but his father was pure Afro-Cuban – '

'And,' said Freedom who had appeared in the doorway, 'my mother was pure aphrodisiac. Come on men, let's go.'

It was not such a bad life after all, George thought. Indeed, taking everything into account, it was really quite pleasant, not at all what he had anticipated when he had first entered the research institution on the outskirts of Chelmsford which had been his home for the last six months. The food was tolerable and, though it wasn't as varied a diet as he was accustomed to, there was no doubt that he was thriving on it. Possibly he had even put on too much weight, but that was more likely to be due to the less strenuous life he nowadays led. He was, in a real sense, too comfortable for his own good. What they said was proving to be true: that once you started to work for the Government the fight for survival in the world outside seemed curiously remote. Here you had your place, did your job and received a proper reward. There was none of the scramble for status that there was outside, none of the frenzied and relentless activity that occupied every waking minute if rivals were not going to undermine your position and with it the whole point and purpose of your life. None of that kind of thing here, thought George. Here you soon settled into the daily routine, knew your place, knew too that it would take an upheaval of unthinkable proportions to alter the status quo. There would be neither improvement nor deterioration in one's life, just the same old thing, day after day. That was the chief drawback, thought George. Boredom. Life outside, no matter how rough, was never boring.

What George was missing, he realized with more than a little surprise, was the rat-race. This was not surprising as George was a rat. He was the oldest rat in Professor Redhill's research laboratory, a large, plump grey accustomed to being waited on front and back and becoming intolerably smug and complacent. Sometimes he suspected they put something in his food that gave him a bellyache, but it never lasted long. Sometimes they picked him up and pushed a needle into him. This neither surprised nor discomforted him, for it was nothing compared with the incision made by a lean and ambitious sewer rat anxious to improve his quality of life; one who had to be shown instantly that he had bitten into more than he could chew. George was being inspected, that is stared at, by Professor Henry Redhill and Richard Bendigo.

'It seems incredible to me, Professor,' said Bendigo, 'that with all the resources of modern science and the State behind you, you are still unable to find a simple and effective method of killing these comparatively small animals.'

George looked at him thoughtfully and scratched behind his right ear.

'Small they may be, Minister,' said the Professor, his residual German accent curiously overlaid by a faint Iberian rattle, 'but they are also highly intelligent. That is how they have survived in such numbers. Man has never beaten the rat in the whole of history. On the contrary, there have been many times when the rat has very nearly beaten man. Hamelin may be a legend, but its real significance is the light it throws on mankind's fear of rodent supremacy and the price mankind is willing to pay to ward off the menace, even to the sacrifice of its children. At the very best we have maintained a precarious balance of power.'

'Balance?' questioned Bendigo who always found that at some stage in any conversation he had with the Professor, there came a moment when he experienced a profound irritation at Redhill's way of suggesting that he knew the answer to everything. 'And the solution to nothing,' he said aloud.

The Professor looked puzzled. 'What?' he asked.

'Nothing,' said Bendigo. 'What I meant was it looks to me as if they are winning.'

'For the moment,' agreed the Professor, 'the rat is in the ascendant. But only for the moment. I am convinced that we will come up with something that will deal with him – for the time being at least.'

'Only for the time being?' asked Bendigo, 'not once and for all?'

'It would take a very naïve person to believe that,' said Redhill, delighted that, impotent though he was, he could still demonstrate his superiority over a politician. 'We will never eradicate them entirely. But never fear Minister,' he said with condescending reassurance, 'we will find something that they will not find an answer to for several generations – say ten or fifteen years.'

'Hasn't your work with the drug companies produced any results?' asked Bendigo.

'Sure,' said the Professor. 'They've produced some very interesting substances and we have been trying them out.'

'With any success at all?'

'It depends on what you mean by success.'

'Do they kill rats?' said the Minister, impatiently.

'Sure they kill rats,' said the Professor. 'Especially some of the slimming compounds they have been working on. Highly effective rodenticides, even in small quantities.'

'Well then?'

'The rats won't go near them. Even a hungry rat. They have to be forcibly administered. Somebody's got to hold their mouths open while someone else shoves it down their gullets and if you put it in normal food they crap on it.'

'Never mind the details, Professor,' said Bendigo. 'I understand.'

'There are also some new beauty preparations,' said Redhill.

'And?'

'We got a lot of sweet-smelling rats, but the only partial success was a depilatory which rendered some completely hairless. They are, however, healthy in every other respect. Sure they tend to catch cold in the winter and feel lousy for a day or two but the problem of getting the lotion to the rat's epidermis is quite a poser – and the results are not very satisfactory when you've got it there.

'My own belief is that the answer will not be found either through ingestion or epidermally but through a greater understanding of the factors that govern both heredity and immunity. We are here dealing with the forces of evolution itself.

'You see, Minister, it is a fact of life that genes and chromosomes mutate all the time. The rate may be very low – one in fifty million or it may be higher, depending on the rate of environmental change on a geological time-scale or on the level of radiation.'

He chuckled. 'Let a few atom bombs go off and you quicken things up like nobody's business.'

He once again adopted his lectern style. 'Most mutations are harmful and do not help the host body to survive. Therefore they die out before they can be transmitted to future generations. But some mutations confer characteristics which make the orgasm – sorry, organism – better fitted to survive. These are passed on. All we know so far is that resistance to each of the historic rodenticides is controlled by a single gene. This means that when a rat with this gene dominant mates with a rat without one, half the resultant progeny will inherit the gene and will also be immune to that particular poison. If the mating takes place between rats which both have the gene all their progeny benefit. Unhappily, Minister, rats do not have any social inhibitions against practising incest. They do not, as you politicians might put it, give a fuck about who they give a fuck. So if half the rats from a single litter mate among themselves, as they tend to do . . . you get the picture Minister?'

'But I thought Darwinian evolutionary theory was dead and done for years ago,' said Bendigo.

'You mean that business in the Bible belt?' Redhill laughed contemptuously. 'Sure God was resurrected for a little while and it brought out some other crackpot notions too. We had clouds of basic life forms floating through space, either blown there by God's breath or hanging about till we bumped into them, we had fundamental creationists who believed in the account of Genesis – who believed in both accounts in Genesis – and there was the view that the real purpose of survival is to provide the gene with immortality and that the human body is merely the transport it has devised for its comfort and convenience. I don't really mind being a passenger in an aircraft whether you call that aircraft evolution or God. I don't even mind not knowing where the aircraft is going or whether it will get there. The journey's not so bad and, occasionally, there's a nice view out of the window. But, Gott in himmel, I'm not going to be the aircraft itself.' And Redhill slammed the bench with his fist making George jump.

'But is it so unlikely?' asked Bendigo. 'I mean, I

can see why it's unacceptable, but that doesn't make it impossible.'

'No,' said Redhill reluctantly. 'It is not all that unlikely. It's more likely, for instance, than Dimnitzer's theory that we are a large battery farm established by a group of livestock breeders from outer space for future consumption. But look at it this way. You're on board a ship and you find out that your most boring cousin is also there. You spend half the voyage trying to avoid him and the other half trying to get to know the beautiful blonde who's making it with the first officer. Then disaster strikes. There's an explosion or an iceberg or possibly both and the ship starts to sink. You are lucky and you are alone in a boat with a pair of oars. One hundred yards to your left you see your cousin waving for help and one hundred yards to the right you see the blonde. Who do you save? Is it the girl whose genes are totally different from yours or your cousin with whom you must have a few genes in common? If the theory is correct and your body is merely a capsule created by your genes for their own onward transmission it must be assumed they would direct you towards their clone genes in order to double the chances of posterity. But is this what happens?'

'I really hate this cousin?' asked Bendigo.

'You loathe him,' said Redhill. 'You have hated him since you were children when he stole your sweeties; he got a better degree than you and he was – and is – more successful with women. Most of your family liked him better than they liked you. Once or twice you even thought your own parents shared that view. Now, are you thinking of saving him and your shared genes or are you thinking of that beautiful girl, helpless in the sea a few yards away, her clothes torn to shreds by the explosion, that girl who will be eternally grateful if you save her? My personal opinion is that you are thinking of that beautiful girl in the shelter of your manly, life-giving arms.'

'No I'm not,' said Bendigo, 'I'm thinking of the first officer. Where is he? What's the point of saving the blonde if she's going to go straight to bed with the first officer the moment we're rescued?'

'At that moment,' said Redhill, 'the first officer's corpse floats by.'

'I save the girl,' said Bendigo.

'There is also the view,' Redhill continued, 'that God created us only ten seconds ago and stuffed our heads with personal and shared memories of things that have never, in fact, happened. That is a variation on the other idea – that God created the whole fossil record at the same time as he created Adam and Eve, that is about 6,000 years ago.'

'Now why would he do a thing like that?' asked Bendigo.

'To fool us, of course,' said Redhill. 'To have us running around in circles; for a big laugh – how would I know why he'd do such a damn fool thing?'

'There are lots of things that don't make sense,' sighed Bendigo. 'Why choke on that? I've never been able to figure out, for instance, why people eat pizzas. All the same, I thought there was some doubt about evolution.'

'The mechanics,' said Redhill impatiently, 'just the mechanics. The way the thing works, not the thing itself. Of course there are gaps in the fossil record. They make a big thing out of that but it's not surprising. Fossils only map the structure of animals, the exterior changes. There are other things that enable adaptation, things that don't show even in the skin, never mind the skeleton. Look at it this way, Minister, if I showed you the body of a plague rat which had somehow been preserved from, say, 1655 and you compared it with George here, you would see no difference at all. But a genetic examination would show you that great changes have taken place in the rat world, all of which have given George the ability to survive the ingestion of substances which would have blown the plague rat apart with their virulence. Feed 'em to George and he just sits back, wipes his whiskers and asks for more, the furry little bastard.'

The Professor's anger and frustration momentarily boiled over.

'But in a million years or so,' he went on, recovering his lecture-room aspect, 'my successor, assuming he is going to be as stupid as most of my colleagues are today, will look at the plague rat's fossil and the calcified record of George here and not only allocate them to the same period – what's five or six hundred years in a thousand thousand? – but decide that there was absolutely no difference between them. Yet the differences that do exist amount to the difference between life and death.

'Of course, if you believe in God, if you believe that God said, "Let there be rats" and there were rats . . . ' Professor Redhill could not go on, the thought was too upsetting. Besides, could the Minister possibly believe in God? Especially a Science Minister? Why not? he asked himself, wasn't there a Minister of Transport who was loony about the bicycle and didn't a recent Minister of Health take sick and die?

'God?' said Bendigo. 'No, I don't believe in God. I do not think that God is a viable proposition. I would go so far as to state categorically that God does not exist. No, there's no God. At least I think so. I mean, it doesn't look as if there's a God, not a God who actually intervenes in the world, a God who cares. No evidence at all that there's someone looking after us, a great impertinence to believe that if we survive a narrow escape it is because God has stepped in and saved us, that would suggest that we are somehow more worth saving than all those who do not survive, all the children, all the better people who are wiped out. I suppose I'm an agnostic when you get down to it.'

'Ach,' said the Professor impatiently, 'it takes courage to be an atheist. To deny is to defy.'

'Defy whom?' asked Bendigo innocently.

'To defy popular opinion, the voters. You're a politician,' said Redhill, 'otherwise you'd say you were an atheist. What else are you afraid of? Being struck by a thunderbolt? Being punished after you die? Even if you are wrong you apologize and you're forgiven. Could God forgive mass murder and not a little honest disbelief? After all, what's worse – to have no faith or to invent cancer and the cholera bacillus like he did.'

'Voters?' laughed Bendigo. 'My dear Professor, you may know a lot about genetics but you know fuck all about politics. Even the voters who believe in God will run a mile from anyone who mentions him in an election address. They're frightened that the candidate might be sincere enough to believe that he's been chosen to do God's work on earth and that's the last thing they want. We sometimes think the electorate en masse is very stupid and in some things they are, but the one thing they do know is that politics and religion don't mix. Oh they'll take a certain amount of humbug, but the moment they think a politician is serious and sincere about God they lose all faith in him. And they're right. Your ordinary politician, if pushed, will regretfully stick you in jail if you overstep the mark. But if he thinks he's doing God's work he'll shoot you in His name and feel all the better for it. Though I must admit there are few atheist regimes that don't do that as well. But in that case, all they've done is to substitute one religion for another and just given the old God a new name.

'Don't get me wrong,' said Bendigo, who was unstoppable on the subject and would continue to argue with himself long after he had finished arguing with others,

'I'm not saying that all virtue is on the side of the unbeliever, but the death squads are particularly fervent and active when they have been told they are ushering in the millenium. In those circumstances it is philosophically impossible to commit error. Fortunately, this kind of thing only happens abroad. Any British politician claiming he is engaged in bringing in a new world according to the gospel of either God or his alter ego, Marx, always loses his deposit. It's different in Ulster, of course. But there they all claim to be on God's side so it's a mere formality, a kind of grace before shooting.'

'If all that is true,' said the Professor, 'why don't you stand up straight with the atheists instead of skulking with the agnostics and hedging your bets?'

'It's very simple really,' said Bendigo. 'I like to cling to the idea that, just possibly, there is a remote chance that, in some forgotten and distant part of the universe where he has been trapped by a faulty time-warp mechanism for a millenia or two, there is someone who is to blame.'

Professor Redhill considered the proposition for a moment then shook his head.

'This rat,' he said, indicating George, 'is living proof either that evolution is correct or that God is at work constantly modifying his original creations in the light of changing circumstances which, of course, he should have foreseen. It is logically impossible to envisage a god who, having once created all forms of life, would simply allow it to muddle along on its own. No, he either exists and is here or he does not exist. He cannot exist and be elsewhere.'

'Well, certainly,' said Bendigo, 'things are changing all the time. What, for instance, would you make of a young man who can withstand the effects of the Immobilization Gases – all of them?'

'You mean,' said Redhill, 'that he has invented a new kind of gas mask? Very interesting, but not up my field.'

'In my field,' corrected Bendigo. 'No, Professor. Not a new gas mask. He just breathes the stuff in and out as you and I breathe the air we're standing in – and with as little bad effect. At least that's what he told me and I've no doubt he was telling the truth.'

'If you're talking about the long term,' said the Professor, 'the air we're standing in will undoubtedly kill us. In the short term, however, we seem to be able to do it without too much discomfort. If you've got some kind of freak I wouldn't mind having a look at him. The probability is that he's somehow become self-immune. In which case it would have no significance. You got him with you?'

'He's not available at this precise moment,' said Bendigo, 'but we should have him soon. Quite soon.'

'He didn't want us digging about in his chromosomes, eh?' chuckled the Professor. 'Tell him it don't hurt. Just a few tests, a couple of weeks at the outside. Or months maybe, it depends.'

'I tried to persuade him to volunteer,' said Bendigo.

'In the name of God?' asked the Professor jovially.

'Certainly not,' said the Minister. 'In the name of science, in the national interest – but he disappeared. We'll find him in a day or two.'

'You should have tried money,' said Redhill. 'People will do a lot in the name of money. They'll sell their blood or organs. A chromosome or two shouldn't come too expensive, not when their posterity is on the market at £5 a time.'

'What do you mean, Professor.'

'Sperm,' said the Professor. 'Put a student in a corner with a dirty book and he'll give you a test-tube full in no time at all. Of course, he'd do it anyway, for nothing, but, unless you give him money he'd throw it away.'

'I could have been rich,' said Bendigo. 'What do you mean, self-immune?'

'It could happen, I suppose,' said the Professor. 'Give a man small doses of poison over a number of years and you can give him a big dose without any ill-effect. Some medical therapy works that way. But that wouldn't be much use to us: it's a process that is confined to the individual. There's no genetic change.'

'You're sure he wouldn't be harmed?' asked Bendigo.

'Harmed? Not at all.' Professor Redhill was at his most professionally reassuring. For a moment or two he could have been mistaken for a doctor examining a private patient. 'Well, not much anyway. Or at least he would not know he had been harmed, which amounts to the same thing.'

His eyes gleamed behind his thick-lensed spectacles. 'You see, Minister,' he said, 'I have a theory that it is the brain that's behind all genetic change. If I'm right I'll be in Stockholm next year.'

'Holiday?'

'Holiday? What are you talking about, holiday? A Nobel prize you damned fool – sorry, Minister, I forgot myself.'

Bendigo ignored the insult and, in truth, it hardly bothered him. 'A Nobel prize eh,' he said. 'That would be a great honour – the Ministry would no doubt get some credit for funding the research would it not, Professor?'

'Certainly Minister. Without your support and assistance it could never have happened. I'll make sure the whole world knows of the part you will have played in it.'

'But the theory, Professor, what is this theory of yours?'

The Professor hesitated. 'You promise you won't say anything – to anyone?'

'Cross my heart,' said Bendigo, 'and hope to die.'

'What's a cross on the heart to an agnostic?' asked the Professor.

'More than it is to an atheist,' said Bendigo.

'Okay,' said the Professor, 'I'll tell you. It's like this –

we all know that bodily functions are controlled by the brain. One part controls speech, thought, the higher processes: another part controls the motor functions, muscle movement etc: a third part looks after the automatic necessities such as breathing, the digestive processes and the pumping of the heart. Why should the manufacture of genes and chromosomes not be controlled by the brain as well? And if that is so why cannot we learn to control this process so that the brain can be stimulated to produce superior genetic material at will, just as I can put electrodes into your head that will impair your speech or make your muscles move? Why not, eh? Why not? If I'm right it is already happening – the brain reacts to outside stimuli and makes its arrangements accordingly. If this young man's brain has reacted to a polluted environment and induced an actual genetic change in him then my theory is right and that is precisely what the rats' brains have been doing.'

'Then why don't you look at the rats' brains?' asked Bendigo.

'What do you take me for Minister – an amateur?' Redhill allowed his anger room to stretch itself. 'Of course we've looked at rats' brains; we've looked at them until our own brains have practically dried up. We've wired 'em up and put 'em in solution; we've kept them in and taken them out; we've lasered 'em and razored 'em and we still can't find the part that controls the genes.'

'In that case,' said Bendigo, feeling slightly sick, 'why do you think you can do better with a human brain?'

'How the hell do you know, for instance,' said Professor Redhill, 'when an electrode is affecting speech? How do you tell a rat to lift up its right arm when you have switched the points so that the left arm goes up instead? Besides, once you start messing about inside their heads, rats die quickly. They got no stamina.

'No, if what you say is right Minister, and we have had

the successful development in a human being of an aberrant gene – that is one which has not caused disease or mental or physical atrophy – we will be well on the way to a form of genetic control that will make all those guys messing about with human sperm and hampster ova even sicker than they are. Who the hell wants humpsters anyway? No, it could be even more useful to your colleague, the Minister of Social Conditioning and Transport.'

Bendigo felt like saying, 'Let the bastard find his own guinea pigs,' there being no love lost between him and his Cabinet colleague. But he remembered the Cabinet oath the PM had insisted they should all take on assuming office and shuddered slightly at the thought. How stupid he had felt, standing there, holding hands with the Minister of Health and Power on one side and the Home and Housing Secretary on the other and chanting 'All for one and one for all; if we're not, then down we fall; one for all and all for one, that's what keeps us ruling on.'

'Incidentally,' said Professor Redhill, as if he had been reading Bendigo's thoughts. 'That's something I've never been able to understand – why all the Cabinet Ministers have double jobs, sometimes even conflicting responsibilities.'

'Above everything else,' Bendigo explained, 'the PM likes a quiet life. Make everyone responsible for two departments of state and he believes, not without reason, that it cuts down the potential for dissent and argument within the Cabinet.'

'But doesn't the Minister of Health and Power, for example, sometimes have to cope with problems to health caused by the use of fossil fuels?' asked Redhill.

'And why not?' answered Bendigo. 'Who is better equipped to reach a decision which takes all interests into account? But that is only one aspect of the Prime Minister's thinking. He also has a distinct fondness for puns and alliteration which is why the Home Secretary is also Minister for Housing.'

'But why,' asked Redhill, exasperation infecting his voice at this demonstration of the non-scientific political mind which he found both ruffling and repugnant, 'why is the Minister of Justice also responsible for Climate Control?'

'That's very simple,' said Bendigo. 'They were the last two portfolios to be filled. Though I do remember,' he added, 'that the PM made some remark about a happy conjunction of bar and isobar. But that, of course, was off the record. Unofficially, I've heard it said that it is a kind of double non-job in that we cannot really control the climate either.'

But clearly Redhill had lost interest.

'Just where is this jerk with the immunity problem?' he demanded.

Chapter 4

'We'll walk,' decided Clementina, setting off along the two-abreast pavement of a one-way street that cut a canyon through the old fruit warehouse district. Flocks of predator children, streetwise as pigeons, wheeled in and out of the back alleys and cart lanes, alert for advantage and any form of gain. Through the gratings of the cellars, now occupied by the unhoused, drifted wafts of bacon fat and curry fumes and the tinny discords of worn-out transistors. HM and Freedom followed Clementina and Penny as they walked through the warming morning air that was already becoming grimy with the smoke and smuts that hung on the breath of the halitoxic households under their feet.

Clementina broke off whatever she was saying to Penny to shout 'Homes for the people!' in a kind of reflex action.

'Right on,' said Freedom, though he added to HM, 'all the same they shouldn't be there man. No Johns.'

'I suppose they've got nowhere else,' said HM.

'That's true,' agreed Freedom. 'But they still stink. They got no running water either.'

They came to a main road and crossed it. Clementina led the way into a more garish district where blue and red neon tubes feebly competed with the mid-morning sun. Stubble-chinned men propped in doorways lazily inspected them, indifferent to the remote commercial prospect they represented. They passed the window of a sex-shop with its lotions, juices, instruments, devices and plastic models wearing black underwear that promised instant access. A notice on the next doorway proclaimed nude encounters in a topless bar. 'It's fellers,' said Freedom, 'topless fellers, a gay bar.'

Signs and posters shifted uneasily in the slight breeze their promise dimmed by sunlight. 'Swedish films for adults only, hard core porno.' 'Model Tracy, 18, second floor,' 'Striperama,' 'Naked Ciry,' 'Sunset Strip,' 'Girls! Girls! Girls!'

A life-size portrait of a naked girl, beckoning smile on pretty face, one hand welcoming, the other covering the illegal part, invited them into a strip show that was closed. 'She's gone man, these three years,' said Freedom – 'D.O.A.O.D.'

'D.O.A.O.D.?' queried HM.

'Dead on arrival, overdose,' explained Freedom. 'Doaod.' He made a word of it rolling it around his mouth, prolonging the awkwardly placed vowels. 'It's the same as dead,' he said, 'only deader.'

A cinema advertised a double bill of 'Schoolgirl Vixens,' and 'Diary of a Teenage Nympho'. A delicatessen exhaled cheese smells and pickled cucumber and the garlic-laden breath of a counterful of Italian salami. An open cavern glowing with lights was already busy with the boom and sizzle of inter-galactic warfare as white-faced boys with multi-coloured hair captained starships and saved the world from alien invaders.

Next to a silent porno bookshop, its windows filled with breasts and buttocks, the doorway of a flat-fronted pub opened to eject a fair-haired man holding a bottle of champagne in one hand and a wine glass in the other. 'Oh do come out ducky,' he called to someone inside, holding the door ajar with one foot while he poured froth into his glass. 'It's lovely and warm.'

His body which had once been well-muscled was becoming flabby and the corners of his mouth were turned down in permanent petulance. 'She simply refuses to venture out into the air,' he complained to Clementina, kicking open the door for her to enter the pub. He let Penny through as well but pulled his foot away to try to stop Freedom and HM following. '*Do* have some champers,' he murmured, a whole tone lower and accompanied by what he clearly thought was a winning smile.

'Don't be silly Terry,' said Clementina. 'They're with me. Leave them alone and I'll tell George to come out and keep you company.'

'Bless you Clem darling,' said Terry, eyes brimming with gratitude. 'You're a positive angel. But I doubt if even your charms will make her change her mind. She's a silly old cow and I don't know why I put up with her. Though she's very fond of you, I must say, all things considered.'

'Stupid old poofter,' muttered a stocky little man who looked as if he had scrubbed his face with a nail brush every morning for seventy years or so. He hurried inside, pushing past HM who was still in the doorway. In a voice dripping with honey, Terry said, 'Oh it's you Alfie dear.' Then, just as the door was closing, he modulated it into a shriek: 'Why don't you go and reinfect yourself, you silly old cunt,' he screamed. HM could still hear Terry's screech of laughter as the door closed. Alfie pushed his way through the crush to the bar giving no indication that he had heard anything at all. But when he got there he turned to the man next to him and said: 'Your mate's making an exhibition of himself again, George.'

'I know,' said George. 'He gets so bored with himself he doesn't know what to do next. Well I'm not going outside to be made a laughing stock.'

'Quite right, mate.'

'Can I get you a little something Alfie?'

'That's kind of you George, make it a Scotch.'

HM was swirled and eddied into a corner of the narrow bar. Clementina had indicated that she would get the drinks and Penny was standing next to him, though they were silent, each thinking his own thoughts. Freedom had been waylaid by a ravaged-looking woman who was being intensely serious.

'That lady,' a voice growled somewhere to HM's right and over his head, 'is a very classy-looking broad.' HM looked up at a tall, blond man with an ageing Aryan face that was pale, even, perhaps, a little grey around the edges. Below it hung a large silver-gilt Star of David on a chain, half inside the open neck of a black silk shirt which, lower down, lost its loose, casual look to stretch tightly across a swelling belly hanging over black trousers. 'Almost,' he voice went on, 'as beautiful as you.' The voice which had apparently been addressed to the whole bar, suddenly narrowed and deepened, focusing on Penny. Without pausing for any reaction the blond man looked at Clementina again and called: 'Come over here Clem, I want you to meet a friend of mine.' Then he was addressing himself to Penny again. 'What's your name kid?' he asked. 'There's someone you should meet.'

Penny told him.

'Hello Joe,' said Clementina who had reached them with four glasses of red wine in her hands, not having consulted anyone about their choice of drink.

She stood on tiptoe and the tall man bent down to let her kiss him on his cheek.

'You look great Clem,' said Joe. But his main interest was in Penny. 'Penny,' he said, 'this is the great Clementina, star of stage, screen and politics. Clem this is Penny, isn't she beautiful?'

'Joe,' said Clementina, 'you're so full of crap it's a wonder they don't tow you down the Thames in a barge. This kid is my son's lady so stop trying to make it with her and this is my son HM. HM, this is Joe Fletcher, what they call a voice over.'

'But never,' said Joe, 'a walkover. You've got a wonderful taste in girl friends, sonny. It ain't so good in mothers, but you can't have everything. Mind you, it's true what she said about me, but she missed out a few things. I may be full of crap and I am a voice over. But I am the only metaphysical, Jewish and drunken voice-over in the whole of the business. And your mother and I once made it together, didn't we sweetheart?'

He looked at her affectionately.

'Not that she's as proud of that as I am,' he said. 'I'd be proud to make it with you Penny as well, that's if you ever get tired of this guy.'

Freedom had shaken off the serious woman and had reached their group. Joe Fletcher put his arms around him and kissed him hard on the mouth. 'Freedom you old bastard, where've you been?'

Freedom disengaged himself and said: 'Joe, you're the greatest piss-artist in town.'

'He's a cunt-chaser,' said a morose, grey-haired, grey-faced man, bitter lines etched on his face, who was leaning against the bar, a brandy in his hand. 'He's obsessed by it, can't get enough of it, won't leave it alone, doesn't care who it belongs to or what condition it's in. If it's there he'll chase it.'

He turned haunted eyes on Clementina. 'For that matter,' he said, 'so will I.'

'Hello Gerry,' she said.

'You're right, Gerry,' said Joe. 'But the fact still remains, that you're the biggest cunt I know and I've never chased you, baby.'

He smiled at Penny and HM and put an arm around each of their shoulders. 'One thing you gotta learn kids,' he said, 'is that you must be nice to people even when they don't look so good or smell so sweet. If we're not nice to each other then we might as well pack it all in, all in . . . ' his voice was slurring, dropping, a resonant rumble that no longer rang above the other noises in the pub but merged with them. HM found himself straining to catch the words that came at him, fragmented like signals from space.

'You gotta dig the I-thou like Buber said, bubeleh.'

'And the yin-yan,' said George who had crept up to the outskirts of the group.

The big man snarled at him. 'Don't you give me that kind of crap, man. See what he's trying to do kid,' – he had turned to HM again – 'I am telling you this because you look like a good kid to me – '

Alfie had also joined the group.

'He's fucking pissed again,' he said dispassionately.

'Listen to me HM – what kind of fucking name is that? – I'm talking to you on account of your beautiful lady and your amazing fucking mother. The lesson is sonny – '

'You listen to him,' said the bitter-faced Gerry, looking as if he would unhesitatingly kill HM if he didn't. 'He knows what he's talking about. He's about the only fucking one in this place that does. Including me,' he added, unconscious of the philosophical complications of his statement.

'The lesson is sonny,' the blond man continued, 'never try to hustle a hustler.' He paused, allowing the message to sink in. 'You remember that,' he went on, 'and you'll be all right. Won't he Freedom?'

And he gave Freedom another kiss, though he had never once taken his eyes off Penny.

'What,' asked HM, 'is a voice over?'

'An actor who has sold out to commercial interests,' said Clementina.

'I put over the message in the commercials,' said Joe. 'For that you need a voice that makes the housewives randy and tells the men that they too could be manly if they would only buy the product. You have to have a voice that's full of mystery, imagination, resonance and timbre.'

'He's an artist, man,' said Freedom, admiringly.

'He's lovely,' said George, fondly.

'He flogs chocolates on the telly,' said Alfie, bluntly.

'He gets away with bloody murder,' said Gerry, bitterly.

Clementina looked at her watch and said: 'I think it's time to go now,' and, without pause, turned and led the way out.

The last thing HM heard was Joe's shout of, 'Remember kid, never hustle a hustler.'

Terry was sharing his champagne with a youth with spiky hair dyed in strips of green, gold and pink. 'I admire the teenagers of today,' he was saying as they went past. 'They are not afraid of expressing their personalities.'

Clementina led them around the corner, across the road and into another pub, much bigger than the one they had been in and very different. It was full of music and the clash of tills with an overworked bar-staff serving beer and bangers, shepherd's pie, Cornish pasties, g-and-ts and lasagne verde.

Clementina led them through a door marked private up a staircase skimmed with threadbare carpet and into a large, gloomy, Victorian room where three men sat around a table far too big for their needs but hardly big enough for the litter of empty beer bottles, full pint tankards, dirty plates and, in the centre, a large oval platter which still contained two chicken legs and some slices of cold beef.

Roger Fawcett, editor of '*Privateer*', the self-proclaimed fearless buccaneering fortnightly, looked up as Clementina, Freedom, Penny and HM entered the room and shouted: 'No lunch today! No lunch today!'

Clementina coolly sat down and picked up a leg of chicken.

'Nonsense,' she said, taking a bite. 'There's plenty of lunch. You're already on the pudding.'

This was undoubtedly true. Indeed, Ponsford, a plump satirist, was virtually in his pudding, one hand encircling it in case someone should try to steal it, the other attacking it vigorously with a spoon and shovelling it into his mouth which had a rim of custard.

Cavendish-Ballantyne, a leading member of the Militant Marxists, who saw the magazine as an instrument for destroying society so that it could be rebuilt after his fashion, said: 'Have some wine.'

This could be interpreted as a preliminary move in the implementation of the decision reached at a recent two-day conference of the Militant Marxist executive, held in Cavendish-Ballantyne's Wapping cottage, to seek an end to the schism which had abruptly shattered the common front against fascism in which the Militant Marxists, Clementina's Reconstructed Trotskyists, the International (anti-Soviet) Communists and the Marxist-Trotskyist-Leninist-Stalinists of Great Britain had joined so effectively. Their most notable victory had been the triumphant conclusion of the Fulham bakery strike which had resulted in six van drivers being fined for breaking the picketing laws. Collections for the Fulham Six had resulted in more than enough money to pay the fines though there was one man who refused to contribute on the grounds that he refused to believe Fulham was capable of scoring six no matter who they were playing.

Freedom and Penny had sat down on either side of Clementina. HM hovered, uncertain of what to do, the only other vacant chair being next to Ponsford who was squinting at him ferociously over his pudding and oozing custard.

'Thanks,' said Clementina, who had heard rumours

that a rapprochement was on the cards and who had been instructed by her executive committee, after a three-day debate, to take preliminary steps to explore any overtures and report back. 'But,' she added, 'I don't see any wine.'

'There isn't any,' said Fawcett.

'Then it wasn't very civil of you to offer it, Fawcett,' Clementina rebuked him.

'I didn't,' said Fawcett, not unreasonably. 'It was Cavendish-Ballantyne. And come to that it wasn't very civil of you to sit down without being invited. This is a private editorial lunch to decide this week's policy. Our weekly lunch to informants when we ply them with liquor in order to loosen their tongues isn't until tomorrow. You can come then.'

'Tomorrow will be too late man,' said Freedom.

'I meant,' said Cavendish-Ballantyne, who always felt an urgent need to explain himself, 'that if you wished for some wine we could order some.'

'So they mean it,' thought Clementina, but she said, 'We haven't come here to drink wine.'

Ponsford swallowed an enormous helping of pudding and, custard gleaming yellowly at the corners of his mouth, said: 'If it's too late tomorrow it's too late today.' Exhausted, he plunged his spoon back into the pudding.

'What he means,' said Cavendish-Ballantyne, who also had a compulsion to explain other people, 'is that as we don't come out until next Friday it makes no difference whether we are told something today or tomorrow.'

'It will make a very big difference if my son here is lying dissected on a capitalist laboratory slab tomorrow,' said Clementina, rising from her chair in order to make the maximum impact.

Fawcett too got up and walked over to the window where he could see the street signs and hear, faintly, the explosions of distant stars in conflict.

In his own way Fawcett was a religious man, though

for sure not of the kind filled with loving kindness and charity. Indeed, he tended to hate most people on principle and wished more for hell for them than heaven for himself. He had chosen this area for his office because it fulfilled his need to have a target for his loathing permanently in front of his eyes as if he feared that in the absence of one his hatred would turn inward. He lived in a southern county but even there tended to face north whenever possible.

'Why should he want to do a thing like that?' asked Cavendish-Ballantyne.

'He doesn't,' snapped Penny impatiently. 'It's them. The scientists and the politicians. They want to see what makes him tick.'

Ponsford, who was nodding, eyes closed, over the empty pudding bowl in front of him, sat up with a start. 'And does he?' he cried.

'Does he what?' asked Clementina.

'Does he tick, of course,' said Ponsford. 'Tick tock, tick tock. Hickory dockery dick, the mouse ran up his prick, the prick struck one and she was done, hickory dockery dick. That wasn't too bad for the spur of the moment, was it?'

'That was terrible,' said HM, opening his mouth for the first time.

'And who was asking you, young fellermelad?' said Ponsford. 'Laboratory specimens should be seen and not heard.'

'It *was* terrible,' confirmed Clementina. 'One what?'

'One what what?' asked Ponsford, looking puzzled.

'You said "The prick struck one". One what?'

'Oh that one! Well, "she was done" so it must have been a girl mouse, mustn't it?'

'Of course,' said Fawcett. 'Any fool can see that. It's not a homosexualist mouse, is it Ponsford? A mouse poofter? One of the gay fraternity?'

'Certainly not,' said Ponsford. 'All my mice are hetero-sexualists. If anyone as much as suggested that they were not perfectly straight mice they would immediately institute an action for libel.'

'And much good it would do them,' said Fawcett.

Freedom thought it was about time someone took his picture so he gave the camera to HM who obliged to Ponsford's astonishment.

'Aren't we getting off the track?' asked Penny.

'You're quite right,' said Cavendish-Ballantyne who had a natural distaste for frivolity of any kind. 'What do you mean by dissected, Clementina.'

'Cut up man, cut up,' said Freedom.

'I am familiar with the term,' said Cavendish-Ballantyne, trying but not entirely succeeding, in keeping the sharpness out of his voice, being very conscious that he was talking to a man of darker pigmentation. 'I know what dissected means. What I do not understand is why it should apply to this young man here.'

'It is very simple,' said Clementina. 'My son here is an evolutionary hero who has discovered how to survive all sorts of poisonous atmospheres. Richard Bendigo, the Minister of Science and Lotteries, found out about it last night while HM was staying with the Minister of Culture. Now Bendigo wants to hand HM over to a Professor Redhill who is an expert on genetics and is head of rat research. It seems that the two things may be connected.

'That is absolutely fascinating,' said Fawcett.

'I don't see what's so fascinating man,' snapped Freedom. 'It's bloody diabolical.'

Fawcett, for the first time, betrayed an interest in HM. 'You mean to say,' he said, 'that you actually spent a night in Dikey Dora's flat?'

'If you mean Dora Dodd,' said HM, 'I suppose the answer must be yes.'

Fawcett whistled. 'That's one for the "It's Happened at

Last" section. I never thought our boring Minister of Culture would ever do anything that would get her into that column.'

'I never thought,' said Ponsford, 'that any column would ever get into our boring Minister of Culture. You mean you actually shafted her?' he asked HM.

'Certainly not. I never said anything of the kind.'

'You mean,' said Ponsford, 'you never said anything of the unkind.'

'No I don't,' said HM, who by this time was beginning to get very impatient with the conversation.

Fawcett rebuked Ponsford. 'You might just as well say – as we have on many occasions – that the private parts of our public persons are their own affair.'

'Public persons have no private parts,' said Ponsford. 'I thought that was our policy.'

'So it is,' said Fawcett. 'But it is also our policy to say that it isn't.'

'But it's not true,' said HM. 'I didn't sleep with the Minister. I slept on a couch in the living room. I couldn't get home. Penny here – ' he stopped, not wishing to add any truth to the scandal.

'Penny here, I suppose,' said Fawcett, 'slept with the Minister. But we're not interested in that. It's well known that Dora is a homosexualist. What is news is if she has taken a young man to her bed which is clearly what happened, despite your denials. What makes you think you know so much about it, anyway? We're the experts in this kind of thing, aren't we Ponsford?'

'Of course we are, Fawcett.'

'So that aspect of the affair is settled then,' said Fawcett. 'There is, of course, this little matter of human dissection.'

'Yes, what are you going to do about it?' demanded Clementina.

'We will take a very strong line,' said Fawcett. 'We will

tell the story exactly as you have related it to us, more or less, and then go on about those fools and nincompoops who have let the greatest scientific discovery of the century – of the millennia – slip through their silly yah boo fingers because of the monumental incompetence of the boring Minister of Science and thingummy, Bendigo. Ponsford, we'll have to think up a new and apposite name for him, something satirical.'

Ponsford wrinkled his brow in thought. HM looked at him with curiosity; he was the only man he ever remembered seeing who had a layer of fat between his eyebrows and his hairline.

Eventually, Ponsford said: 'How about ratface?'

'I can't see – ' began HM.

'Then you shouldn't look,' said Ponsford.

HM ignored him. 'I can't see how this can possibly help me to stay undissected,' he said.

'It's quite simply really,' said Cavendish-Ballantyne. 'The first priority – as Clementina understands full well and would acknowledge if she were not acting under the influence of maternal feelings – the first priority is to get rid of the turds who form the present government. Anything which will help us to accomplish this is immensely useful. In this way Clementina, your son can be of even greater benefit to the nation than if he were laid upon a laboratory table and had his intestinal secrets ripped out of him.'

'It seems to me,' said HM, 'that all you are saying is that I should be dissected by someone else.'

Cavendish-Ballantyne was genuinely puzzled. 'Surely,' he said, 'you are capable of seeing that there is a fundamental difference between being a victim of the capitalist system and a willing participant in the forward march of mankind?'

Freedom's basic pragmatism burst out impatiently. 'You may be right man,' he said, 'but what if you do change the government? You think the others are just as bad as this lot don't you?'

But HM was looking at his mother who, in turn, was looking at Cavendish-Ballantyne with a respect verging on admiration. It was clear to HM that she thought he had made a good point.

Ponsford said: 'Bad? They'd be a damn sight worse.'

'Exactly,' said Cavendish-Ballantyne, and when the people realize that they will take the only step logically possible, they will turn to us.'

Fawcett laughed mirthlessly. 'You lot, over the shop in Balls Pond Road?' he said. 'All eight of you?' He rolled a mouthful of slim-line tonic around his mouth and added: 'You could be right at that.' He and Ponsford subsided into a deep gloom which Ponsford sought to relieve by scraping the pudding bowl and licking the empty spoon.

Penny broke the silence. 'I don't think,' she said, 'that the revolution will come quickly enough for HM to be a willing participant in the forward march of mankind even if he wanted to. So if we are going to prevent him from becoming a victim of the capitalist system instead, hadn't we better do something?'

Her question was addressed to Clementina who pulled herself together. 'You are quite right Penny,' she said. 'Some people just believe in sitting on their arses and waiting for revolution to happen simply because the alternatives have failed. Others believe in action.'

So the rupture in the forces of the Left was not to be healed at this stage, thought Cavendish-Ballantyne, and the onward march was once more to be halted simply because of the fissiparous and schismatic nature of those comrades who, while agreeing about the ends, could not co-operate on the means. Dear God, when would they find unity? Christ Almighty! How could he even think such a thing as 'Dear God!'? Would he never shake off the religious imagery of his upbringing. Jesus wept! He was at it again. This must stop at once. He must learn to say 'fuck me' like a proper worker.

Clementina thought: that's put a stop to him. I'll call an executive committee meeting and get my rejection of his approach confirmed. Aloud she said: 'I think we'll go and see Marcus Markovitch.'

She led the way out, HM bringing up in the rear of the small procession. As they were leaving he heard Fawcett say: 'They're going to see that yid.'

'I wish you would not use that word,' said Cavendish-Ballantyne irritably. 'It's totally unjustified. Markovitch is not even a Zionist.'

'Some of the best yids are my friends,' said Ponsford.

'Are you accusing me of anti-semitism?' demanded Fawcett, turning on Cavendish-Ballantyne.

'Of course he isn't,' said Ponsford, trying to make peace. 'Everyone knows you like Arabs.'

Professor Redhill was not quite sure who irritated him the most – George with his sleek whiskers and amused expression or the hirsute Borash, his assistant with his long hair, full beard and tufts of the disgusting stuff bristling from his nostrils and ears. It was Borash, he decided, Borash who listened so politely, so disbelievingly to all his ideas about the possibility of programming genetic change by locating the area of the brain responsible for the manufacture of genes; Borash who was sceptical about the basic premise of the brains having any say at all in the production of genes. And yet why not? Wasn't the brain responsible for all the activities that took place in the depth of the body, from the higher ratiocinative functions to the regulation of the circulatory and oxygenating mechanisms? And had not Eastern mystics demonstrated over and over again that the brain could be trained to control such things as metabolic rate and body temperature over which some Western scientists, Borash included, believed it had no power whatsoever? It was not as if this had been done by training the brain to take over a function with which it had not previously been concerned; rather it was the discovery of the yoga practitioners that it was possible to control those areas which the brain had always commanded at a deep level of the sub-conscious and to create such an awareness of the process that it was possible for them to lower their metabolic rate as easy as it was to raise an arm. Once that was accepted, it followed that there was little doubt that the brain was also responsible for the manufacture of genetic material and that once the right area had been located some control could be effected, not by pure thought but by electrodes. In this way the whole world would benefit. People just could not be expected to be able to call on the tremendous intellectual concentration demanded by the higher disciplines of yoga. A proper, repeatable, scientific discovery, however, was available to everyone; mankind could change its whole future. That, thought Redhill, was the difference between a scientist and a mystic. The mystic said: 'Follow me, but find the way yourself'; the scientist said: 'I will find the way and you will be able to follow'. On the whole, the world seemed to prefer the scientist; mystics were not awarded Nobel prizes. Just give him a shot at a brain – particularly one that had a highly developed potential for fundamental genetic change – and watch out Stockholm. That would show Borash with his stupid, negative approach; always going on about the international convention on genetic engineering which had virtually put a stop to all progress in the field – except, of course, in those countries which had ignored it even if they had signed. All because that idiot Krankenhammer in Zurich had insisted on publishing photographs of his sheep with a baby's face, or was it a baby with a sheep's face? Whatever it was, the whole world had gone mad.

Krankenhammer had been proud of it too and amazed at the public reaction. He always had been a great fool, thought Redhill.

But the immediate problem was this fat, sleek rat in the cage. The Professor was only half-listening to Borash's report on the latest experiment. But one look at George was sufficient to tell him that it had failed.

'We gave him fluorocetimide last night,' Borash was saying, 'and this morning he breakfasted on arsenious oxide and arsenic tri-oxide.'

Redhill looked longingly at the fire axe hanging on the wall. That, he thought, would kill him for sure, would wipe that supercilious look from those bright, inquisitive, healthy eyes.

'Try the thalium sulphate, Borash,' he said at last.

Borash, for once, allowed the mask to slip and, despite all the hair, alarm registered on his face.

'Surely not Professor,' he stammered. 'Not the thalium sulphate. You know what happened to Woodbine with the thalium sulphate.'

'Woodbine is a fool,' snapped Redhill and, seeing that Borash was about to correct him, corrected himself first. All right, *was* a fool. If you use the protective clothing and the vacuum pump you will have nothing to worry about, nothing at all. But don't forget the vaccine, just in case. Woodbine thought he was indestructable. A vain and conceited man. That was a wonderful memorial service we gave him.'

'But – '

'No buts Borash. If you delay me with your silly arguments I shall have to explain precisely why to the Minister. I am due at his office in less than ten minutes. He's meeting a deputation from the Royal Society for the Prevention of Animals or something and wants me to be there. They want to discuss cruelty to animals. You'd think at a time like this they'd have more to do than worry about cruelty to rats. Who's being cruel anyway? Look at that rat, the picture of health. I should feel like he looks. When I return I want to see that rat dead. From thalium sulphate poisoning.'

On the way to the office of Marcus Markovitch, Penny, Clementina and Freedom tried to explain to HM who Marcus Markovitch was.

'Marcus believes in the expansion of consciousness through Marxism,' said Freedom.

'He aims for a synthesis between dialectical materialism and transcendental meditation,' said Penny.

'He believes in the expansion of Marxism through consciousness,' said Clementina firmly. 'The elimination of capitalism by the art of Zen.'

'The eradication of poverty by astral farming,' said Penny.

'And an increase in circulation by tit pictures,' said Freedom.

Markovitch's office lay up three flights of rickety wooden stairs in an alleyway off St Martin's Lane. Clementina, without knocking, walked straight into a small room dominated by a large desk covered with layout sheets, photographs, drawings, diagrams and plastic cups containing dried-up or still mouldering dregs of caff-type coffee. The walls were covered with posters devoted to astrology, phrenology, meditation, Hare Krishna, occultism and gay pop groups. A gaunt-faced man with haunted, hollow eyes was seated at the desk looking at a garish layout displayed by a fair-haired youth who stood over him, one hand on his shoulder, the other pointing to some feature on the page.

Markovitch rose when Clementina and her retinue entered and greeted her with formal politeness, waiting so expectantly to be introduced that Clementina found herself obliged to act the society hostess. HM found

Markovitch's speech almost incomprehensible. Later, Freedom told him that he had been taken by his parents from a religious school in Lithuania to a Belfast tenement and the resultant mixture of accents had forced him into a literary career as he was unable to communicate verbally with anyone and had no gift for music. Once, in a desperate attempt to find someone to talk to, he had returned to Lithuania, but even in his home town of Vilna, he had been treated as an incomprehensible foreigner.

Being so isolated from society, Markovitch suffered greatly from the world's inability to synchronize its mental and moral watches. His whole adult life had been spent in pursuit of the common factor which would bind together all the disparate elements which he perceived in society and which, he discovered, were reflected in himself. As he contained a central, binding force, an ego which imposed a kind of peace on all the warring factions, he adduced that a similar power existed outside and that it was his business to find it.

The fact that he had not been successful so far in no way affected his belief in its existence. The whole thing had started in his troubled adolescence in which it had only slowly dawned on him that the beautiful thoughts he was expressing were ninety per cent pure gibberish to everyone except his mother and father. His mother could understand him but never listened; his father listened and then told him that everything he said had already been better and more beautifully expressed in the Hebrew holy books.

There had been a minor homosexual experience, which he had rather enjoyed, in a cubicle at a public swimming bath with a man who said he owned both a motor cycle and a yacht but whose socks had holes in them – something which Marcus, an observant boy, had noticed – and, a few weeks later, an incident with one of his friends' sisters in a disused air-raid shelter just off the Falls Road which gave him his first orgasm.

He had been sent to Hebrew classes where he was taught by a Russian dissident who, having learned Hebrew in order to emigrate to Israel, had found, when he at last got there, that deep down inside he was still a Communist. Unable, like most of his friends, to re-emigrate to America on political principle, he had turned up in Belfast with nothing to sell except his two languages though his career as a teacher was gravely handicapped by his lack of English.

While Marcus was thus exposed to the Hebrew language, in which he was already fluent, and Communist ideas every evening from five to six and every Sunday morning from nine to twelve, Mr Devlin, who took him for history, English and woodwork at his comprehensive school, was an old-fashioned laissez-faire Liberal who believed in the universal panacea of free trade conducted without any government interference of any kind with market forces.

Marcus had thus grown up to be sexually and politically ambivalent, a believer in both the dictatorship of the masses and in the rights of the individual; he also believed in dialectic materialism and telepathy, that Judaeo-Christianity was a superstition both separately and together and that astrology had a scientific basis. Most of all, he believed that to all these apparent irreconcilables there was a simple unifying factor which, when applied to the economic, political and social scenes, would bring peace between Jew and Arab, Ulster Protestant and Catholic, Communist and Capitalist, Fascist Left and Fascist Right, Muslim and Buddhist, black and white, black and brown, brown and white, brown and brown, black and black, white and white, men and women, cops and robbers, cowboys and Indians and, though he never admitted it to himself even in his most introspective moments, between him and his father – his mother having died long since – who was now eighty-five years old and living in a religious home in Stamford Hill.

Markovitch listened attentively to HM's story, told by Clementina who had by now worked out all the right pauses and stresses and was giving a superb performance of anguished motherhood. When she had finished Markovitch pressed his index fingers together and said: 'It is a disgraceful story. I will give you the whole of the centre spread. It will arouse the nation.'

The assistant whispered something in his ear which HM could not catch.

'I'm sorry,' said Markovitch. 'Not the centre spread. We are committed to an appeal to allow serving naval officers the same homosexual rights as civilians – '

' – Equal Rights for Gay Sea Dogs,' said the fair-haired young man, proud of his headline.

'There is, however,' said Markovitch, 'a large space on the front page.'

'Oh Marcus,' said the assistant, 'you've forgotten. It's pre-empted.'

And he bent down to whisper again in Markovitch's ear.

'I'm sorry,' said Markovitch. 'It seems I promised the front page for an analysis of signals from the region of Alpha Centauri. It rather looks as if an intelligent life force is trying to contact us.'

'Oh Marcus!' shrieked his assistant with a moué of anger. 'You should not have said anything. That is an exclusive story.'

'I'm sure our friends will not tell anyone,' said Markovitch with a winning smile, all the more attractive because of its obvious rarity. 'There is also the regular photograph in our series "A modern guide to the Kama Sutra".'

'Not a word man, we won't say one single word,' said Freedom.

'I'm sure you won't,' said Markovitch. 'And I'll be able to devote the whole of the next issue to this alarming development.'

'That's wonderful,' said HM. 'When will it be coming out?'

'It's difficult to say really,' said Markovitch. 'So much depends on the advertising. If we were coming up to the Body and Soul Exhibition at Earls Court I'd say next week, but as we're not it could be about six weeks.'

The assistant whispered something again and Markovitch amended his words. 'Seven,' he said.

On the pavement outside Clementina said, 'Harvey Hall.'

Freedom whistled as he handed her his camera and put an arm around HM's shoulders. 'Right on,' he declared. 'Harvey Hall's on the ball; a guy with real muscle.' He turned to HM to explain: 'Special Investigative Journalist Harvey Hall. No detail omitted. Harvey Hall's the fly on the wall.'

'He always used to lunch at the Happy Bulgar,' said Clementina, 'and late as well. If we hurry we'll just make it.'

Harvey Hall was as neat, as compact and as self-contained as a pocket watch. Whereas most people have something that seems to be attached to them rather than a part of them, a mop of hair, a nose, their clothing – Harvey Hall was all one piece. His neat grey suit, his small leather-shod feet, his precise hair, his straight sharp nose, all matched, complemented each other, toned or balanced. He never made a statement that could not be verified, never made a judgement that could not be justified and never entered an argument he couldn't win. Clementina only had to say two sentences for him to grasp the basic elements of the story and invite all four of them to join him for lunch. A waiter stood poised attentively for the order.

'I suggest,' said Harvey Hall, 'a Grosdova each to start with. A Grosdova is made from the debris of the grape after the wine pressing. All the stalks, pips and skins. It is a colourless spirit, something like grappa. Only a little rougher.'

'Perhaps the lidies would prefer a sok,' suggested the waiter.

'A sok,' said Harvey Hall, 'is a fruit juice made from peaches or plums, or sometimes a mixture of both. It is non-alcoholic and very sweet.'

'I think I would prefer a Grosdova,' said Clementina.

'Me too,' said Penny.

'I think,' said Harvey Hall, 'that we will start with some kiopolo – egg plant and peppers with garlic.'

'Five kiopolo,' said the waiter, busy writing.

'And then I suggest pulnee pee perkee. Pulnee pee perkee is stuffed cabbage.'

'We have some sarmee sus neso,' said the waiter. 'Ver' nice.'

'Vine leaves with minced meat,' explained Harvey Hall.

'Or posnee sarmee.'

'Cabbage rolls with rice. Set in calves' foot jelly.'

'With some bope,' the waiter said, getting into his stride.

'White beans boiled with onions, paprika, tomatoes and mint.'

'To follow – Banitas.' The waiter's cry was triumphant.

'Cheese pie like strudel, only made with cheese. Goats' cheese, of course,' said Harvey Hall.

'And to finish,' said the waiter, 'I suggest – '

'Revenes – '

'A traditional cake made of walnuts and orange rind, drenched in syrup.' And he stood to attention, pencil poised expectantly.

'I think we'll leave it to you Harvey.'

'In that case,' said Harvey Hall to the waiter, 'make it the usual five times.'

By the time they reached the revenes and were on the traditional glass of accompanying prostike ('a liqueur made from rowanberries' explained Harvey Hall) Clementina had finished her story and HM had repeated it in his own words. Harvey Hall had a notebook out and seemed to be taking down every word.

'What were they wearing?' he asked HM.

'Who?'

'The two ministers of course. It's detail like that that makes the piece interesting.'

HM tried to be helpful. He concentrated on recalling the scene at Dora's flat. Eventually he said, 'The Minister of Culture wore a suit and the Minister of Science a kind of cardigan.'

'What colour?'

'Blue. Dora's suit that is. Mr Bendigo's cardigan was a kind of beige.'

'Beige cardigan,' muttered Harvey Hall, writing it down. 'That's very good, a domestic touch. He is still plump, balding, aged fifty-two, isn't he?'

'Yes, yes and I don't know,' said HM. 'We didn't discuss his age.'

'Don't worry, I can check as soon as I get back to the office. Now what did the Minister of Science and Lotteries – we always give ministers their full titles – actually say?'

'He said,' said HM, who felt that he had already disclosed more than he knew, 'that he wanted to get me into Professor Redhill's laboratory so that they could run some tests.'

'Yes I know that,' said Harvey Hall patiently. 'What I want is some detail of the conversation, the actual words used, to flesh things out a bit. Adds to the authority of the piece. Makes it look as if we were actually there, a fly on the wall.'

Freedom slapped his knee and Clementina shushed him.

'He told me I'd be famous – '

' – actual words please.'

'He said, "You'll be famous and you'll be the answer to the nation's most pressing problem".'

'But how was he in himself, I mean was he pleased or upset or what?' asked Harvey Hall.

'He seemed a bit sad if anything,' said Penny to break the ensuing silence as HM desperately tried to recall the impression he had never in fact registered of the minister's feelings. Penny went on: 'He went on a bit about his day being over and that he and everyone else would be superseded by HM.'

'He called me weedy as well,' added HM, hoping that this was what Harvey Hall wanted. He was rewarded by the journalist making a note.

Then Harvey Hall did a momentous thing. He put his notebook in his pocket and carefully capped his ball-point pen and slid it inside his jacket.

'There is no doubt about it,' he said. 'We will save you from Professor Redhill. There's not the slightest doubt that for the Minister to restrain you and forcibly hand you over to this laboratory for scientific investigation is contrary to every single one of the provisions of the Safeguarding of the Person bracket non-molestation by public bodies unbracket Act passed last year after our investigations into the Barraclough scandal.'

'The Barraclough scandal?' interjected Clementina. 'What was that. I was away filming most of last year in Jugoslavia. We didn't get much English news there.'

'Barraclough,' said Harvey Hall, 'was a cleaner at the Ministry of Defence and Rural Development. One day he picked up a piece of paper from the floor and found it was the chemical formula for a new and highly offensive weapon. There was no question about his loyalty, but the new drugs perfected by the Americans, the Russians and the Chinese are capable of recreating in the memory everything that the eye has ever seen, even if the brain did not understand it. If these drugs were combined with the Swiss revelation drug – which they are selling to anybody who cares to buy – it meant that not only would he be able to remember the formula but that he would be unable to resist the most ordinary request and would therefore blurt it out to anyone who asked. It means that spies need no longer carry cameras for they can look at something and then take the total recall drug when they get back to their base. Their controls can even check that they have not been turned by giving them the revelation drug to see if the two accounts match up. It also means that it is no longer necessary to torture captured agents or suspects. Except for pleasure of course.

'Anyway, the Ministry kept Barraclough captive while they tried to think of a way of dealing with the problem. After a while though he managed to smuggle out the famous message.'

'And what was that?' asked Clementina.

'It was addressed to us, the Investigators, Sunday Probe and it read: 'Help. I am a prisoner in the Ministry of Defence and Rural Development through no fault of my own. I am a true-born Englishman and a cleaner. Yours truly, R Barraclough".'

'And then what happened?' asked HM.

'We ran the story of course and questions were asked in the House and Barraclough was eventually released. There were calls for the Minister's resignation but the Prime Minister said that although an error of judgement had been made no real harm had been done and no useful purpose would be served by taking such a course. After all, it had been a matter of the nation's security.'

'Didn't anyone get fired?' asked HM.

'It did not really seem necessary,' said Harvey Hall, a

little testily. 'It was not as though the Minister had even been told of what had happened.'

'What happened to the chap who dropped the paper in the first place?' asked HM.

'Wasn't there still a security problem?' asked Penny.

'Oh yes,' said Harvey Hall. 'There is to this day. Barraclough is accompanied everywhere he goes by three armed special branch men with orders to shoot without hesitation should it ever become necessary.'

Clementina was clearly about to become indignant. 'That is simply barbarous,' she said. 'Do you mean that if a couple of friendly Russian officials or tourists happen to approach this ordinary man in the street, this cleaner, to ask directions or something they would be shot?'

'Certainly not,' said Harvey Hall. 'It's Barraclough who would be shot.'

'It's still disgraceful,' said Clementina, unwilling to waste a good head of outrage. 'The threat of death is going to hang over that poor man for the rest of his life.'

'Not really,' said Harvey Hall, 'the information will one day be obsolete or the Russians will get it in the usual way, through the technical press. Once that happens he'll be able to lead a normal life again.'

'I bet he'll be a lousy cleaner,' said HM. 'He's not going to be so keen on picking up bits of paper for a start, is he? But I still don't see that it's got a lot to do with my case. I haven't got anything in my head that I could tell anyone.'

'I wouldn't be so sure,' said Harvey Hall thoughtfully. 'Professor Redhill, you say? If I remember rightly I once read a paper by him in some obscure scientific magazine. I think he was arguing that it should be possible to develop a technique for the conscious manipulation of genes. He said the main difficulty in the way of research was the sheer impossibility of experimenting on a live human brain. But of course, if he is being backed by a department of state he may not find that to be such a problem after all.'

'My God!' said Clementina. 'The bastards!'

'What can you do about HM then?' asked Penny.

'You realize, of course, that there's a book in this,' said Harvey Hall. 'The last one we did was top of the best-seller list for fifteen weeks and was translated into twenty-three languages. You'd do quite well out of it,' he reassured HM. 'We usually give the subject a straight two per cent of royalties, net, that is, not gross. Of course we'll need your collaboration. The Minister was right in one respect. If what you say is true then you are unique and of great scientific interest. What you must do is to place yourself in the hands of our scientific experts and we'll look after you. After all, we can't have you roaming the streets can we? If the Ministry doesn't get you, the Globe will and where would we all be then? You know what things are like between the Globe and the Probe.'

HM stood up and said, 'Excuse me, can you tell me where it is?'

'Where what is?'

'The loo.'

'Through there,' said Harvey Hall motioning to the back of the restaurant.

HM thanked him and as he left the table he saw Harvey Hall pull out his notebook and pen again and turn to Clementina. 'Was he a normal baby?' he asked.

He never returned to the table.

Chapter 5

A number of changes had taken place in Professor Redhill's laboratory. George was still there, sleek and plump as ever, his whiskers sharp and shiny as needles. But instead of a cage he now inhabited a glass case. A window had been cut into the wall above it, and to its right, but no light streamed in, for it looked into another room, a room to which an airlock door further along the same wall gave access. A small platform had been built below the window, presumably for the Professor who would have been unable to see through it without its help. Between the window and the doorway a bank of television monitors pulsed, blipping light and bleeping sound. Most of the signals were regular, steady pulsations of energy giving clear indications of a rhythm of life. One or two were as erratic as the flight of gnats, darting over the screen with seemingly random spasms of green flash which left traces of phosphorescence wherever they had been.

Redhill was standing on the little platform, his gaze veering between the window and Bendigo who was looking with fascination at the flickering screens.

'You have had him for a month now, Professor,' said the Minister. 'Any results yet? Is he all right?'

'All right? Of course he's all right, Minister. You can see for yourself.' He indicated the television monitors. 'Pulse rate, temperature, respiration, brain activity, metabolic rate – all normal. But results? After only a month? That's far too early. We cannot rush things when we are dealing with such sublimely delicate matters as those areas of the human brain which function in as yet unknown ways.'

'I can't tell if he's all right from these bloody television sets,' said Bendigo. 'Some of the signals seem to be all over the place.'

'Perhaps to the non-scientific eye,' said Redhill condescendingly. 'But even the most seemingly erratic signal, if looked at long enough, will take on a regular pattern.'

'I know,' said Bendigo. 'It happens just before I fall asleep. I've noticed it at home, too.'

'So come and have a look at him through the window, Minister. It's all right; he's not aware of us. To him it's just a mirror.'

Redhill laughed very unexpectedly. 'Mirror, mirror on the wall,' he cackled, 'Who is the rarest of them all?'

Bendigo was uneasy. Just how mad was Redhill? He had long ago concluded that most of the scientists he had to deal with were, to some degree or other, short of their full complement of marbles, but it had been decided that the only ones who needed full-time surveillance were those engaged on chemical and nuclear research. True, Redhill was partially chemical but their sparse resources were strained to the limit and it was felt that virtually the only damage he could do was to rats. Maybe the risk status of the rat-research laboratories would have to be re-examined, thought Bendigo. He made a mental note to discuss it with Blantyre, his chief of security, tomorrow. Blantyre had set up M.I.Sc., the Ministry's intelligence section, on orders from the Prime Minister after the Barraclough case. High-risk projects had been pinpointed after it was discovered that the whole ridiculous Barraclough mess had been created by a laboratory assistant in some obscure research centre in Hounslow who thought he had invented an antidote to the Swiss revelation drug but had run into a few administrative delays in getting it tested and acknowledged. After a mere eighteen months he'd gone off his rocker and apparently dropped a number of secret chemical formulae in the corridors of the various ministries he had visited on the conducted tours arranged under the Freedom of Access Act. Sooner or later some wretched nonetity like Barraclough was bound to pick one up. Of course, once the report on the crazy scientist's grievance had reached his Ministerial desk, Bendigo had ordered the drug to be tested, principally on Barraclough. It had worked wonderfully well, the cleaner's mind not only having been wiped clean of the formula he had accidentally seen but of any recognition of numbers or their meaning. Unhappily for everyone – but particularly for Barraclough as things had turned out – his guard had had to be retained because to withdraw it would have alerted the Soviet Union or, even worse, Fleet Street. The mad laboratory assistant himself had been silenced by condign threats and extravagant promises of NATO contracts, but if there had been one more public scandal, one more Ministerial witch-hunt with the Minister cast as witch and accusations of blundering and red-tape thrown all over the place – but mainly at him, Bendigo – the Prime Minister would have jumped up and down and stamped his little feet and he would never have heard the last of it. As things were, every laboratory that was considered to be at risk had been quickly infiltrated by Blantyre's M.I.Sc. men who had found it relatively easy to recruit science students while still at university. They had either been concerned about their job prospects after graduation or had volunteered on ideological grounds once, that is, they had been given the impression that they were working for the Chinese. Blantyre's original idea to fool them into belief that they were working for the Russians had not worked, the Kremlin having become more distasteful than even 10 Downing Street to the current crop of revolutionaries.

Barraclough himself, an inoffensive man whom he had met once and liked, had not really been inconvenienced by his 24-hour guard – had, in fact, been helped by them when he boarded the wrong bus, as he frequently did, being unable to read the numbers – until that very morning when extreme action had had to be taken.

It was not until several days later that Bendigo was told that the group of bearded men in long, black overcoats and wide-brimmed hats who had approached Barraclough as he was walking to work down Whitehall, were not Russians but pious Chasidic scholars from Stamford Hill who wanted to know where the Home Office was in order to present a petition begging that their leader should be permitted to display the Royal Coat of Arms on his attache case in recognition of the fact that he had circumcized five Royal children in as many years.

The bodyguard, mistaking the Chasidim's appearance, language and intentions, had to the utter consternation of onlookers and, for that matter, the victim himself, shot Barraclough stone dead as they approached him. Fearing for their own lives, the Chasidim fled, not stopping until they were safely in Stamford Hill, and the contingency cover-up plan devised by Blantyre had immediately swung into action. The gun-shot and blood were explained away by a statement to the effect that an American tourist had been injured rather seriously when his electronic camera had exploded as he was filming a mounted trooper on Horse Guard's Parade. The horse had reared up inflicting further injuries. The trooper had been thrown off and falling head first, the spike of his helmet had pierced the American tourist's chest. The tourist would return to America when he recovered and disciplinary action would be taken against the trooper as soon as possible. Later it would be given out that Barraclough had died of a heart attack at his home in Balham. The newspapers, busy interviewing the American tourist's 19-year old honey-blonde daughter (one of M.I.Sc's best operatives), would not connect the two events.

Much later, Bendigo heard through an operative Blantyre had placed in a kosher salami factory, that the Chasidim had believed that the whole incident had been contrived in order to punish them, and their leader fashioned many a homily on the theme of the unwisdom of placing trust in princes. All the same, the next time the Palace sent for him he went.

But on the day that Bendigo had been told that Barraclough was dead his immediate thought was that with that embarrassment finally out of the way the manpower problem in M.I.Sc. would be eased. He wondered if one of Barraclough's bodyguards – he vaguely felt that this, possibly, was not the right word – had sufficient qualifications for him to be able to be placed in Redhill's laboratory. This was unlikely, he gloomed as, on the whole, they were a pretty bone-headed bunch.

Bendigo did as Redhill had bid him and, standing on the little platform, looked through the window. The room in view had been comfortably furnished with a reasonable number of chairs, a divan bed, a dining table and well-stocked bookshelves. A television set stood blankly in one corner and Bendigo could see a tape-deck and a rack of tapes. Two doors at the far end of the room were slightly ajar, one leading to a kitchen, the other to a bathroom.

Although he was prepared, it was still something of a shock to see the young boy he had last seen eating Dora's sandwiches and drinking Dora's whisky, lying on his back on the divan, a magazine and two books by his side. He was not reading however; simply staring at the ceiling. Bendigo found it difficult to believe that if HM just looked up he would not see him through the window.

'Well, what do you think?' asked Redhill cheerfully.

'He looks comfortable but bored,' said Bendigo.

'Bored? How can he be bored? He has everything a

young man could wish for, a nice room, plenty to eat and all my books to read. There are others as well.

'He's a damn sight better off even than our friend here – ' he indicated the rat – 'and he lives the life of O'Brien. I saw to it all myself, personally. Nothing but the best, the very latest equipment. No old-fashioned electrodes for him. Everything is monitored by sensors which follow him wherever he moves, each one picking up a different signal from his body – pulse rate, perspiration, respiration, blood pressure. I tell you there's nothing we don't know about that boy. If he reads a sentence that upsets or moves him we know about it and we can relate it to the scanners that not only watch him but watch what he is watching.'

'I can't see any cameras at all,' said Bendigo.

'Of course not. They are part of the light fittings,' said Redhill triumphantly. 'We analyse his body wastes within seconds of their evacuation and everything is instantly shown on the monitors while, at the same time, a full record is being kept.'

'That last monitor doesn't appear to be very active,' said Bendigo, turning away from the window, vaguely uneasy about watching someone who was unaware of it.

'That,' said Redhill, an unmistakable note of pride in his voice, 'is the best of all. My own invention, or rather,' he added modestly, 'my own modification of existing technology. You see, Minister,' he went on, 'sometimes the subject of an experiment such as this appears to be absolutely normal, suffering no ill-effects whatsoever. Later, we discover that, for some reason or other, there has been a loss of sexual drive. Everything else is OK – blood pressure, heart, waterworks, everything. You'd think that when people are locked up on their own they'd think a lot about sex. Not so. If anything, they tend to think about going for long walks.

'At least all the literature says so. I've had no experience of locking anything up except rats and who knows what they think about. Probably about eating you if the look in their eyes is anything to go by.'

He paused as if his mind had gone off on another train of thought.

'So?' Bendigo reminded him gently.

'So?' queried Redhill.

'So what did you do about it – this lack of sexual drive, this diminished libido.'

'You know it? You know the word?' Redhill was astonished.

'Certainly,' snapped Bendigo. 'I may be Minister of Science but that does not mean I am a complete scientific ignoramus.'

'Well then,' said Redhill, 'you'll understand why I call this monitor a libidogram. I thought it was a good idea if we kept an eye on his libido.'

'A libidogram? How does it work?'

'How else?' said Redhill. 'It records his erections of course.'

Bendigo found that he couldn't take his eyes off the blank screen.

'And so far?' he said at last.

'So far,' said Redhill. 'Nothing.'

'Maybe your device isn't working properly.'

'Impossible. It has been thoroughly tested. I'll let you into a little secret Minister. When a climax is reached that little bell you see over the monitor, rings.'

His smile was conspiratorial. Clearly he was going to let Bendigo into a secret that, secretly, he was happy to tell.

'I myself,' he said, his voice dropping as if he didn't want George to hear, 'have rung the bell twice this month.'

He paused while he peered closely at Bendigo's face to

gauge the effect of what he was saying. 'Not that I would go into details, eh Minister? But not bad for a man of my age, you must admit.'

'But Professor,' said Bendigo, forgetting the implications of his next remark in his sheer amazement. 'You're only in your mid-forties.'

The smile on Professor Redhill's face froze and then slowly disappeared. It was like watching water going down a partially-blocked drain. Eventually he said: 'You mean twice a month is not good for the mid-forties?'

Bendigo said nothing.

Redhill, his subject forgotten, sat down in a plastic and chrome chair and buried his face in his hands. He said something which Bendigo strained to hear.

'I always knew,' Redhill was saying, 'I shouldn't have gone into a profession which meant working with all these lousy chemicals.'

He looked up and strode back to the window.

'But when I was his age,' he shouted, pointing at a point in the wall beyond which, Bendigo supposed, HM was located, 'it was happening all the time. I remember . . . '

'But there's not much stimulus in a laboratory,' said Bendigo, hoping that it would explain both HM's inactivity and Redhill's inability.

'Stimulus? I didn't need a stimulus,' shouted Redhill. 'Just riding a bus was enough. And thoughts. You saw a lady and you got a thought. You thought of a lady and you got another thought. Sometimes you got a thought when you didn't even think of a lady. I couldn't get it out of my head. Even now . . . '

Bendigo was sympathetic. He knew how Redhill had felt when he was young. Maybe Redhill was the more fortunate of the two of them after all. He felt like the way Redhill was describing every day.

'There's a girl friend,' he said. 'She keeps asking me to let her see him.'

Redhill laughed mirthlessly. 'See him? Do you realize Minister that she would die the instant she set foot in that room. Maybe after the first series of tests has been completed – it's amazing the number of different atmospheres you can think up – maybe then she could be allowed a visit. But there must be no break in the sequence, no exposing him to normal air. In two or three more weeks perhaps.'

'You mean to say,' gasped Bendigo, 'that that is a poisonous atmosphere in there?'

Redhill laughed, mirthlessly. 'Poisonous? You heard about the bacteria that live in the New Zealand sulphur springs?'

Bendigo nodded.

'They wouldn't last five minutes in there,' said Redhill.

'But how does he survive?'

'That's what we're working on,' said Redhill. 'My assistant Borash has got some crazy idea that he's from the planet Venus.'

'Nonsense,' said Bendigo. 'I know his mother. But how do you know that he's going to survive these other atmospheres that you say you're introducing.'

'We don't,' said Redhill. 'But every time we introduce a new one we have a team standing by with oxygen masks. The slightest gasp from our friend in there and they'd be through that airlock and have him out before you could say Jack Watkinson.

'But so far we have not had reason to call on them. That boy can breathe anything. My assistant Borash will bear me out that we take every possible precaution and that so far – ' he searched frantically around the room for a piece of wood to touch without success – 'there's never been a moment's danger. To him, that is. Borash is another matter. Where is that fool? Just because he's had a little accident – that's no reason to neglect his duties. Borash! Borash!'

He was still screaming for Borash when Borash entered the laboratory. At first Bendigo did not recognize him. Borash was completely hairless; head, chin and cheeks glistened pink and smooth; even his eyebrows, Bendigo noticed, were missing, and his eyes were unrimmed by lashes.

'Where've you been?' Redhill demanded. He turned to Bendigo and shook his head. 'He's not been the same since his little accident.'

'What on earth happened?' asked Bendigo.

'It was entirely his fault,' said Redhill. 'No one else was to blame. It was his mistake and he admits it, don't you Borash. He signed a paper,' he added triumphantly.

'All I did was sneeze,' said Borash. 'And that's what I admit. I sneezed.'

'All he did was sneeze,' repeated Bendigo, derisively. 'All he did – ' he laughed. 'At the wrong moment, though, wasn't it Borash?' He turned to Bendigo and in a pitying voice said, 'Just as he was preparing the vapour.' But the pity in his voice was more the pity of contempt than of sympathy. 'That is no time to sneeze,' he went on. 'Even a little cough at such a moment is not wise. Still,' he continued briskly, 'he's better off than Woodbine. A snuff-taker,' he explained. 'Mein Gott, that was terrible. Next time Borash you may not be so lucky.'

'Was the – er – vapour for the – er – subject in there,' asked Bendigo, 'or the rat?'

'For the rat,' muttered Borash.

'And what happened?' asked Bendigo.

'Like mother's milk to him,' said Redhill. 'Like a fresh wind blowing in from over the sea. He breathed it for half an hour and then went off and screwed a lady rat. Soon there will be more baby rats and when they grow up they'll all screw each other. And they will be able to breathe air that would wrinkle up the skin of your finger if you put it in. That's the trouble with rats – they've no social or sexual inhibitions – sisters, mothers, brothers, grandmothers, males, females – if it looks like a rat they'll screw it.'

'You mean,' said Bendigo amazed, 'that there are gay rats?'

'Sure there are gay rats,' said Redhill. 'If the females in a colony are depleted for some reason or other, homosexuality catches on like wildfire. They go at it like knives.'

'I would have thought,' said Bendigo, 'that in this proclivity may lie a partial answer to our problem. I mean, if the number of rats with such preferences could be increased by some method, it would soon mean an end to the population, wouldn't it. I mean, no copulation, no population.'

Redhill looked at him pityingly. 'There are some problems in getting homosexual rats to reproduce themselves,' he said. 'In that respect at least they are not like humans. I mean, in the rat world, heterosexual parents usually have heterosexual children. It's odd, when you come to think of it, that it's not the same with us. But that's by the way. What we did was to produce a strain of gay rats through artificial insemination. We had quite a thriving colony at one time.'

'What happened?'

'What happened is that we got a lot of very frustrated and angry lady rats. And one thing we did find out Minister that we didn't know before but perhaps should have guessed is that one angry and frustrated lady rat does ten times more damage than a happy, satisfied lady rat. For a start she eats more, much more. Never stops eating. You think you got trouble now Minister? Believe me, a frustrated and angry lady rat is not something you would wish your worst enemy to meet in an alley-way on a dark night.'

Bendigo considered the idea. 'Oh I don't know,' he said, thinking of one or two of his political opponents and several of his colleagues.

He was still musing on the prospect when there was a sudden disturbance at the door, a scuffle, a voice protesting, 'but you can't go in there, the Minister's there with the Professor.' He turned round as Penny burst into the room. Once inside she stopped abruptly and looked at the three men.

'Good God Penny, you can't come in here,' said Bendigo.

'I want to see him Richard,' said Penny. 'You've had him for a whole month now and you keep promising but nothing happens. What have you done to him?'

Without waiting for an answer she turned to Redhill. 'You,' she snapped. 'Are you in charge here? Or is it this hairless monster?' Borash shrank under the fierce contempt of her eyes and voice.

'I am Professor Redhill, if that's what you mean,' said Redhill, but he was thinking, 'If she calls him Richard they must know each other pretty well.'

'Is he still alive?' Penny demanded.

Bendigo's feelings were deeply hurt and his voice mirrored them. 'Of course he's still alive,' he said. 'We're not murderers you know.'

'I don't know any such thing,' retorted Penny. 'And anyway, you're experimenting on him. He could be in diabolical pain. Torturers!' She screamed the last word so loudly that Borash jumped and Bendigo paled. Only Redhill was unmoved.

'My dear young woman . . .' he began.

'Don't you dare talk to me like that,' screamed Penny.

'All I was going to say was that he could be in diabolical

pain but he's not. Equally, he could be in Birmingham but he's not; he's here.'

'You poisonous dwarf,' hissed Penny. 'I want to see him. Now!'

'But you can,' said Redhill. 'All you have to do is to stand on that little platform there and look through that window.'

Penny darted towards it and peered through the glass. She waved and smiled excitedly. Then she tapped on the window and called out: 'HM! HM!' She turned to Redhill, her passion regenerated. 'Why can't he see me?' she demanded. 'Why can't he hear me? You've made him blind and deaf.'

'Nonsense,' said Redhill wearily. 'There'd be no point.' He turned to Bendigo. 'I suppose this is the young woman you told me about,' he said. 'The subject's mistress.'

'For God's sake Redhill,' said Bendigo, 'don't call him "the subject". He's a human being.'

'Not to him he isn't,' shouted Penny. 'To him he's just a subject. Why can't he see me?'

'Because he can't, that's why,' said the Professor tartly, 'and the answer is perfectly simple. The room is soundproofed and the window you are looking through isn't a proper window but a one-way glass. On his side it is a mirror on the wall. That's all there is to it.'

Bendigo was relieved that the Professor had not repeated his 'Mirror, Mirror on the wall' piece.

As an afterthought, Redhill added: 'And it's perfectly possible to be a subject and a human being at the same time. That rat is a subject,' he said, pointing to George. 'Yet he is undoubtedly a rat as well, a rat named George as a matter of fact by my assistant here. Didn't you Borash? Call him George? Who after I don't know. But I suppose it gives him some kind of anthropomorphic identity such as weak minds require. It is odd, is it not Minister, that a human subject in there should be known only by his initials even to his loved ones whereas the rodent subject in here has a proper Christian name?'

'Very droll,' snapped Bendigo who was in no mood for philosophizing of this nature.

Penny stepped down from the platform and said, 'I'm going in to talk to him.' She made for the airlock door.

'You can't Penny,' cried Bendigo, 'it's just not possible.'

'Isn't it?' said Penny purposefully. 'Just watch me.'

Before anyone could prevent her she strode over to the door and turned the handle. Bendigo's hand went up to his mouth in horror. Borash and Redhill hadn't budged. 'It's locked,' said Borash.

'Open this door,' demanded Penny, rattling the handle.

Redhill said: 'How did this crazy girl get in here? How did she get past the guards?'

Penny pulled a card out of the back pocket of her jeans and flourished it at him.

'Open the door,' she demanded imperiously. 'I have a pass to go anywhere I please.'

Bendigo walked over to her and looked at the pass which she kept still for him but kept firmly clutched in her hand.

'Not here you haven't,' said Redhill. 'This is a restricted area. That means that if you try to get in you get restricted.'

'It's signed by Dora,' said Bendigo. 'I mean the Minister of Culture. She's made Penny her personal assistant.'

'This is not a cultural establishment,' said Redhill. 'The Minister has no authority here. Her pass is worthless.'

'You forget about her other portfolio,' said Bendigo. 'She's also Minister of Works and Public Buildings which gives her the authority to enter any government building in order to assess its decorative needs. Or any person so designated by her,' he added to make it quite clear.

'She's still not going into that room,' said Redhill. 'Experimental laboratories are excepted.'

'That is not an experimental laboratory,' said Penny. 'It is an ordinary bed-sitting room and I'm going in whether the pass is valid or not.'

And she seized the fire-axe hanging on the wall and before any of the men could stop her she swung it at the handle of the airlock which shattered under the impact.

'Don't Penny,' shouted Bendigo, moving towards her. 'It's dangerous. You'll be killed.'

She swung the axe at him, narrowly missing, and he shrank back.

She pulled what was left of the handle and the door swung open. The three men started coughing and spluttering but Penny darted inside.

'Quick Borash, the door – shut it!' yelled Redhill.

Borash leapt to the door and slammed it tight. He leaned his weight against it.

Bendigo shouted: 'Change the air. She'll die in there.'

Redhill was at the window. 'It's too late,' he said. 'She's inside already. There's no time.'

Bendigo found himself rushing between the airlock door against which Borash leaned, immovable, and the platform on which Redhill stood. 'How long has she got?' he cried. 'We've got to get her out.'

He made for the door again.

'Stop him Borash,' ordered Redhill. 'If we lose the Minister we could lose the grant. Stop him.'

'She's too young to die,' cried Bendigo, his eyes brimming with tears as he stood irresolutely between the two men. 'Too young and too beautiful.'

'She's too stupid to live,' said Redhill brutally. 'Anyway, nothing can save her now. There's one thing Minister, it will be quick. She will go over like this.'

With his hand he indicated a sudden collapse.

'In about ten seconds – four, three, two, one. That's it.'

Bendigo's legs weakened and he slowly sank to his knees. 'So she's dead then,' he said, more to himself than to either of the others. 'That beautiful young girl, dead. She was so alive, so full of spirit. All gone. I can't bear to look.'

'All the same,' said Redhill who was once again at the window, 'come here and look.'

'Is she in pain?' asked Bendigo. 'Is she suffering? If she's still alive, can't we get her out. What about the guards with gas masks?'

'They're only available when we change the atmosphere,' said Redhill. 'On our grant we can't have them standing by twenty-four hours a day. Just come and look Minister. A very strange thing is happening.'

'What is it,' moaned Bendigo, 'is her body dissolving? That beautiful, young body?'

'It could be,' said Redhill. 'But at the moment she's kissing him.'

Bendigo rushed to the platform and in his haste knocked Redhill aside. 'My God you're right Professor,' he gasped.

Penny and HM stood in the middle of the room locked in an embrace.

Redhill had joined him on the little platform and was looking through the window. He put one arm around the Minister's rotund waist to stop himself falling off. Bendigo was embarrassed both by Redhill's body pressed against his and the sight of the embracing lovers.

'What does this mean, Professor?' he asked.

'I think they like each other,' said Redhill.

'I gathered that,' said Bendigo. 'I mean why is she not dead like you said she was?'

'Like I said she should be,' corrected Redhill. 'There is only one answer and that is – Quick, the door!'

Bendigo saw that Borash had slumped against the door he had held shut and was slowly sliding sideways away from it. 'He's fainted or something,' shouted Redhill. 'Go and hold the door. I can't leave now.'

Even as he spoke his head was veering rapidly between the now loose airlock door and the spectacle on the other side of the window. Bendigo ran over to the door and, pushing the limp body of Borash aside – he noted that he was still breathing – sat down on the floor, his back pressed against the door.

'Good,' said Redhill. 'We don't want any more of that nasty stuff in here do we Minister?'

'I still don't understand,' said Bendigo. 'What is happening in there?'

'In fact,' said Redhill, 'there is only one possible answer.'

'You mean,' said Bendigo, getting to his feet, 'that the atmosphere in there is not deadly after all. There was some mistake.'

'Get back, you fool,' screamed Redhill. 'Get back. Sorry Minister, I shouldn't have said that. But you got a whiff of the stuff yourself didn't you? Two whiffs and your hair would fall out – what's left of it. Three and your teeth would go. Four and your legs drop off. Five and there wouldn't be anything left to live for. Look at Borash. What do you think's knocked him out. He was nearer the door than you were, that's all. No, can't you see what the answer is? She's immune too. We don't just have one freak but two freaks to work on now. A male freak and a female freak. That's pretty freaky, I can tell you. We must hear what they're saying. Don't move!'

He dashed from the dais and turned a dial before hurrying back to the window. Penny's voice filled the room. 'Are you sure you're all right?' she asked. 'Everyone's been so worried about you.'

'A bit bored, that's all,' said HM. 'But nothing's

happened to far except for a few funny smells. I just sit here and read most of the time. The food's not bad and every so often they let me out for a walk in the grounds. With a chap called Borash. He doesn't say much. I expect they're keeping me under observation for the time being. Did they tell you when the experiments would start?'

'No they didn't,' said Penny. 'But you're not waiting for that; we're going to get you out of here.'

'There are armed guards everywhere,' said HM. 'There hasn't been a chance of escape since they picked me up.'

'Clementina and Freedom are working on it,' said Penny. 'There's a petition and they're seeing lawyers. They're talking about a writ of habeas corpus or something but it's a question of whether that's still available under the new Freedom of the Individual Act. Don't worry HM, we'll get you out soon. In the meantime, I'm staying.'

'Will they let you?' HM asked.

'They'd better,' said Penny.

There was a long silence. 'What are they doing now?' asked Bendigo, bracing himself against the door.

'Just looking at each other,' said Redhill. 'Sitting on the divan and just looking at each other. Like they were hungry. Now she's standing up. So is he. Himmel, she's taking off her shirt. She's got nothing on underneath! Now she's standing there looking at herself in me – I mean the mirror. Mein Gott! She is beautiful. This is not fair, not cricket. I'm supposed to be the observer, Minister, not her. She's looking straight at me. She knows I'm here. What does she take me for – a rat in a cage? Go away young woman, go away! You have no right to do this.'

'But she can't see you or hear you,' said Bendigo.

'I know that,' snapped Redhill irritably. 'But the little devil knows I'm here all right. She's even smiling at me.

Now she's coming nearer; she's unfastening the top of her trousers. Go away! Go away!'

'She can't hear you, Redhill,' said Bendigo. 'It's soundproof.'

'Do you think I don't know that?' said Redhill. 'What kind of scientist do you take me for? I don't forget things that easy. Now she's stepping out of her trousers. Gott in himmel, she's got nothing on under them either.'

'Come away Redhill,' said Bendigo. 'They're entitled to a little privacy at a moment like this. Close the curtains. Turn off the sound.'

'Close the curtains! Turn off the sound!' Redhill was outraged.

'Are you mad?' he demanded. 'This is a scientific investigation, not a Soho strip show. We are witnessing the start of a new evolutionary era, something that has never been seen before in the history of mankind. And you want me to shut my eyes! You think I am doing this out of prurience, for a cheap thrill. Look! I am not moved; I have no erection. Adam has found his Eve and I am watching them take the first bite of the apple. Of course I am excited, but it is a scientific excitement. Close the curtains! Turn off the sound! What kind of Science Minister are you?'

Borash stirred and dragged himself to his feet.

'Good,' Redhill continued. 'I'm glad you've decided to rejoin us Borash. There's work to be done. They're about to mate in there. Make sure all the monitors are working properly. They should be showing more of everything, pulse rate, breathing, body temperature. God, I wish we had her monitored as well. But we will by the next time. Switch on the camera over the divan, that's the obvious place.'

Borash staggered over to a control panel and pressed a touch button.

Redhill let out a Teutonic shout of annoyance. 'She

has spotted the camera over the divan,' he shouted. 'She is putting her trousers over it.'

'That's right,' said Borash in confirmation. 'I can't see a thing.'

To Bendigo's surprise, Redhill turned away from the window, stepped down from the platform and slumped into a chair near George's glass case.

'I'm glad you've seen it my way, Professor,' said Bendigo. 'There are certain things which should remain private I feel, and this is one of them. There are things that are altogether too sacred.'

'Balls,' said the Professor unexpectedly. 'With all respect Minister, balls. She put her shirt over the mirror, the little cow.'

He turned to George in the glass case. 'You wouldn't give a damn if we put your fornication on a wide screen and showed it to the whole world, would you.'

George, aware that he was being spoken to, looked at him inquisitively and twitched his whiskers.

'Sometimes,' said Redhill, 'I think I prefer dealing with rats.'

'Look,' said Borash, 'look at monitor number six.'

The libidogram was clearly working faultlessly. A sharp fluorescent line starting in the bottom left hand corner of the screen was climbing rapidly towards the centre top of the screen. Once there it curved over and descended, the line fading and renewing just on the point of vanishing so that it pulsed with increasing rapidity. Then the silent room was pierced with the clangour of the bell. The three men sat there, each buried in his own thoughts, not daring to catch another's eye. Bendigo himself felt a mixture of shame and awe, though he was not at all sure why. When the bell stopped there was silence for a moment or two. Then Redhill rose to his feet and told Borash to push a heavy filing cabinet against the airlock door, thus relieving Bendigo of his responsibility. 'There's nothing more we can do here, Minister,' said Redhill. 'We may as well adjourn to my office. Borash, organize the maintenance people to repair the lock. In the meantime let no one in. Come Minister.'

They left the laboratory and were walking down the corridor when the bell began to ring again.

Chapter 6

It was clear to Bendigo and to Dora Dodd that the Prime Minister was about to make a speech. When this happened at a full Cabinet meeting it meant that the decision had already been made either in committee or by the PM himself, alone and unaided except for his secretary, wife, mistress – though God knows what they did together, Bendigo had often thought – and his chauffeur in whom, the PM believed, there reposed the collective wisdom of the masses. Whatever the path by which the decision had been reached it was undoubtedly already made. All that the Prime Minister now required of them, thought Dora, was approval and that was merely in order to preserve the fiction of Cabinet responsibility. He might, for form's sake, allow a little discussion, but he would brook no debate.

The Prime Minister ostentatiously waited for the Minister of Sport to finish the story he was telling the Minister without Portfolio whose giggle was stilled by a glare from the PM who then said:

'You have all had a copy of Professor Redhill's report and I assume you have all made some assessment of its implications insofar as the nation is affected in general and your own departments in particular. If Professor Redhill is right in his theory that there are many more of these immunees, as he calls them, hidden within the general population, it seems to me that there are three possible methods of dealing with this extraordinary evolutionary development. Two of these methods call for the location and subsequent isolation of these people. That done, one possible course would be to prevent the further spread of their peculiar genetic make-up by a programme of forcible sterilization and vasectomy.

'The alternative to that is total elimination, a process which would inevitably involve adverse publicity both at home and abroad and which, furthermore, I am assured by my advisers, would be contrary to the provisions of a number of international agreements we have signed, all concerned with curbing the tendency of governments to massacre their own citizens. And that in a possible election year. I stress that I only say "possible", though if word were to get out that I had referred to an election even in those terms it would only throw confusion into the ranks of our political enemies. In short, I would have no objection to a controlled leak on that point. But only on that one please.

'Alternatively, we could encourage the breeding of further immunees as a possible long-term benefit to the community. Should we decide to do that we would have to make conditions as pleasant as possible for them, thus conferring a special status on one section of the community at the expense of others. Since this has been happening from time immemorial I see no special difficulties in that course.

'A fourth possibility is to ignore the whole business and allow nature to take its course. This has obvious attractions but the drawback is that we then lose control of the situation. It might eventually result in the whole population becoming similarly immune or, alternatively, in the dilution of the immunity to the point where it would eventually die out.

'Evolution, so I am informed, has led up many blind alleys before. There was no straight progression from ape-like ancestor to our present advanced condition, but hundreds of variations, some of which survived until comparatively recent times in the more remote regions of the earth such as New Guinea, Papua, South Africa and Ulster.

'But in view of the environmental factor I feel I have to disclose to you information contained in a document circulated between heads of government at our recent summit meeting in Tierra del Fuego. This was to the effect that though the atmosphere was superficially improving because of the passages of various clean air acts, the true situation is that every industrialized society is spreading atmospheric conditions that are affecting the whole world. This, of course, has been known for a long time. As far back as the 1970s it was discovered that the London air contained more sulphur-dioxide than anywhere else in the world, 160 micrograms per cubic feet, well over the danger level. The one reason there was no public outcry, as there had been over the earlier pollution by the burning of fossil fuels – or smoke as it was known then – was that it was invisible. Invisible, but no less dangerous. No remedial action was taken because it would have been vastly expensive. The position, of course, has steadily deteriorated and now the cost of de-polluting the atmosphere is astronomical. Nevertheless, some of the under-developed countries, those that have so far failed in all their efforts to create atmospheric pollution of their own, are beginning to complain that they are getting all the muck and none of the brass, as my Lancashire great-grandfather, the mill-owner, used to say. After all, a case can be made out for poisoning your own population if the profits are high enough to give the survivors a good standard of living, but it is difficult to convince people who are not benefiting that it is necessary for them to perish from pulmonary infections in order that we should continue to have a good time. Yes Foreign Secretary? Or is it Sport you wish to bring up?'

'Speaking as Foreign Minister, Prime Minister, I have already received representations to this effect from numerous Third World countries. But the fact is that those countries with the largest populations have always accepted early death as an unalterable law of nature and, indeed, would be gravely embarrassed economically if their people started setting longevity records. Other Foreign Ministers, those who have demonstrated the greatest anxiety, have indicated their willingness to forget the whole thing if a sufficiently large arms deal could be arranged. The most hidebound of them are willing to overlook a few thousand premature deaths of their own people if they are given the means to arrange ten times as many in military carnage even-handedly distributed between their own and neighbouring populations.

'Now I turn to my major responsibility, Sport, and I must say I can see considerable advantages in having a team of British athletes who are unaffected by poor atmospheric conditions. Even as Foreign Minister, a few international victories would considerably strengthen my hand in the conference chamber.'

'Good thinking,' said the Prime Minister. 'And now I believe the Minister of Education and Fen Drainage wishes to say a few words. Am I right?'

'Yes, Prime Minister, and, if I may say so, as usual. Wot I say is that we should do – '

'Forgive me for interrupting,' said the Prime Minister, 'but I would be glad if you would follow custom and announce in which capacity you address the cabinet.'

'I speak as Minister of Education and wot I say is this, that we should do what's best for this great old country of ours and take bugger all notice of what those foreign fuckers think, if you'll pardon the expression.'

'Certainly, Minister. I think "bugger all" is too commonplace nowadays to disturb even the most delicate nature, but I am sure we all appreciate your sensitivity in thinking of the more susceptible in our midst. Yes Ms Dodd?'

Dora said: 'Does it not mean Prime Minister – and here I speak less as the Minister of Culture and more as a coward – that those of us who are not immune to the effects of atmospheric pollution will eventually die painfully if something is not done to improve the atmosphere now?'

'I hardly think so,' said the Prime Minister. 'I am advised that we are talking about a long-term prospect and that as long as people can get on the moors now and again for a spot of grouse shooting or deer stalking there is no real danger. Things will go on pretty much as they are now with more or less all of us in this room dying in the next twenty years or so, more or less painfully, depending upon the availability of drugs to alleviate whatever condition it has pleased Divine Providence to visit on us. Whereas, if we have to find the vast sums needed to de-pollute our skies, there will not only be considerable hardship to taxpayers – with electoral consequences I hardly need to spell out – but no means of ensuring that other countries will follow our example. As a result, all our efforts could come to nothing with a change of wind, or, as one of my predecessors said, a wind of change. No, we are discussing the legacy we leave our children or, as none of us as far as I am aware is an actual parent, the legacy which we leave our country. Posterity will no doubt judge us, but we'll all be safely dead by then. Rather it is a matter of whether we risk losing power now.'

'As Minister Without Portfolio, doubling as Minister with no special responsibilities, I feel I can speak on both accounts when I say I feel I can take a wider view than some of my colleagues with particular responsibilities. Therefore, Prime Minister, I say we should act.'

To which another voice added: 'As Minister With Portfolio, I concur.'

The Prime Minister settled back in his chair. Dora and

Richard Bendigo exchanged glances. Both recognized the sign. The PM was about to indulge in one of his periodic bouts of whimsy.

He addressed himself to both the last speakers who, as was their custom, sat next to each other at Cabinet meetings and usually played a surreptitious game of noughts and crosses. 'When you say "act" gentlemen,' said the PM, 'may I inquire in what sense you use the word?'

The Minister With Portfolio looked at him blankly. Then turned with mute appeal to his colleague.

'I mean,' said the Minister Without Portfolio, 'that we should do something and not just sit here on our behinds while events take charge of us. For too long, this country of ours has been at the mercy of international forces and . . . '

'Quite so,' said the Prime Minister, 'quite so, Mr Bolsover. I was, in fact, posing a philosophical question as no doubt you appreciate. Do we act in the sense of doing something, or do we act in the alternative meaning of the word – to simulate or appear to do something? Shall we, in short, bring in an Act or put on an act? Shall we, as you might say, be seen to take action or shall we merely convey that impression by putting on a performance, that is, acting? To act is the key verb in politics in that it covers every possible political course from activity to non-activity. A most useful word. Yes, Minister of Education and Fen Drainage? You wish to say something?'

'Yes Prime Minister. And what I wish to say is that actions speak louder than words. That's what I always have said and that's what I always will say. And I can't say fairer than that.'

'Nor indeed you can, Minister,' said the PM. 'No doubt you will also agree that act*ing* speaks louder than words?'

Dora could not keep her impatience out of her voice.

'Can we skip the semantics Prime Minister?' she said. 'How many people will die if we do nothing about the atmosphere?'

The PM was momentarily annoyed but he decided not to indulge his power and, sighing reluctantly, returned to the business before the Cabinet.

'The report of the secret conference of Western pollution scientists – it took place recently in the Windward Islands – suggests that the world population will be decimated in about a century if nothing is done. They were, of course, not using decimated in its original sense of a loss of one-tenth but in its modern, broadcasting usage of a survival rate of one-tenth. As many of the pollution scientists were also going on to a conference on population control – in the Virgin Islands – there was a rider to the effect that this was not necessarily a bad thing. A minority report by those scientists interested in curbing the increasing population was roughly to the effect that they felt that their function was more to try to prevent excessive populations being born rather than wipe them out once they had arrived. But then, as we know, there are idealists everywhere. All Governments concerned have, of course, agreed to keep the report secret. Anyway, it was drawn up without knowledge of the evolutionary development here. Professor Redhill believes that taking that into account some 60 to 75 per cent of our population will survive. It follows that, apart from avoiding an immense and immediate financial – and electoral – burden, we will be in a position of strength vis-a-vis other nations that this country has not enjoyed since Victorian times. It is on these grounds that I am strongly in favour of creating maximum opportunities for increasing the birth-rate among immunees while, at the same time, taking precautionary measures to see that the strain is not diluted in any way. In short, they can only sleep together if they both possess the new gene that the Professor has isolated.'

There was a silence not broken until Dora said: 'Can we seriously envisage the death of 35 to 40 per cent of our people for the sake of a long-term power advantage?' she asked. 'It's an appalling prospect.'

'Hear, hear,' murmured Richard Bendigo, faintly.

'Oh come now, Dora,' said the Prime Minister, 'and you Richard. You know as well as I do that for decades we have envisaged and prepared for a nuclear situation which would result in the eradication of not 35 to 40 per cent of the population but some 99 per cent. You know that the existing deep shelters will protect only national and regional heads of government and those forces that will be needed to maintain a social structure of a kind.

'This factor has never stopped any government in the past from proclaiming a determination to use nuclear weapons in order to safeguard the future of the nation.'

'I have always wondered,' said Bendigo, 'how one can claim to be protecting a nation by announcing that you were prepared to use devices that would eliminate most of the people who constitute it.'

'That,' said the Prime Minister, 'is because, like Dora here, you have never been interested in the way words are capable of infinitely subtle variations of meaning. When you use the word "nation" all you think about is some vague collection of people who share a certain history, certain attitudes and certain aspirations. This is almost certainly untrue as history, attitudes and aspirations among the people of even this small island differ widely. The whole thing falls into place much more easily if you forget individuals and just think of the nation – this or any other – as an abstract entity. Once you do that you will find it perfectly possible to maintain the idea of the continuity of a nation, even if every other member of it, apart from yourself of course, has been wiped out. It really is the thought that counts. But of course, not everyone is going to be wiped out so isn't it better to think of a plan which will ensure the survival of our most advanced and adaptable people rather than all those boring and conformist administrators who will have access to the deep shelters and who would never allow any genetic behaviour except of the most proper kind.'

'I would like to ask, Prime Minister, what proposals you have for the location and segregation of these immunees?' asked the Minister With Portfolio.

'I'm glad you asked that question,' said the PM. 'And I am even more pleased that you – and, I take it the rest of you here today – are agreed that the first priority is to locate and segregate these people. Do I have your agreement that this would be the right and proper course to take. Good. No dissidents – sorry, I mean no dissenters. Thank you all.'

It was not until he was out in the street that the Minister With Portfolio realized that he had not been given an answer to his question about how the immunees were to be located and segregated. The other ministers, all except Dora Dodd and Richard Bendigo, did not even realize that the question had been asked. Dora though, had a few ideas on the subject and as soon as she returned to her Ministry she telephoned the PM's office to ask for an appointment.

Chapter 7

Penny and HM had come to an agreement with Professor Redhill: they would moderate their hostility and perhaps even co-operate a little if they were allowed some privacy in return. 'Bed and bathroom,' said Penny firmly. 'How would you like it if you knew someone was peering at you all the time, even at the most intimate moments?'

'I can quite see,' agreed the Professor hastily, 'that it must be very embarrassing when you are – er – making love. It would put me off for sure,' he added with a nervous laugh.

'I wasn't thinking about that so much,' said Penny, 'as wiping my arse. Though why you should want to watch me do that I don't know. Maybe it turns you on.'

'Oh no,' said the Professor. 'Certainly not. I mean it doesn't turn me on. No. What I mean is that I don't watch you doing that – or anything else like it and if I did it wouldn't turn me on.'

'Then take the cameras out of the bathroom and off the bed,' repeated Penny.

The Professor agreed. Later he told Borash: 'We have the instruments. We must think of ourselves as aircraft pilots flying blind. There's nothing to it these days.'

But I always get sick when I fly, thought Borash.

Penny assumed that there were concealed microphones everywhere so did not even ask for them to be removed. 'It's not really a bad thing,' she told HM, her voice a little louder than usual. 'It means that we can tell those freaks outside exactly what we think of them whenever we feel like it.'

'It's better than that,' said HM. 'If we're as interesting

as they say we are they'll want to show off to other scientists, show them their records. It won't look good if there are gaps in the tape. Which do you think is the bigger freak, Redhill or Borash?'

'Redhill, no question,' said Penny. 'He's a very weird guy when you come to think of it. I think maybe Borash is just a little crazy – but compared with Redhill he's almost normal. I think Redhill has a lot of problems. There's that odd accent of his. German mixed with Spanish. That's a crazy mixture for a start. Especially when he gets excited like when I told him he must like looking at me wiping my arse.'

'When I was talking to Bendigo,' said HM, joining in the game, 'I got the impression that he thought Redhill was pretty sick, not physically of course.'

'Turn that damned thing off,' snarled Redhill to Borash.

'But the record, the continuous record,' protested Borash.

'Fuck the record,' said Redhill, 'turn it off. More of that crap I do not wish to hear. I mean I don't want to hear any more of that crap.' And he himself lunged forward to clip off the switch. 'We've got the instruments. That's all we need. They tell us things about those two before they know it themselves. Us freaks! The nerve! We couldn't live in that room where they are sitting, talking all that garbage.'

So the girl had noticed the South American flavour to Redhill's faint German accent, thought Borash. Henry Redhill, born Herman Rotberg, in Paraguay, son of Klaus Rotberg, importer/exporter but of what the file entry didn't say, and Eva, née Muller. Not much Paraguayan blood there, Borash had thought. So what, all the Nazis were long since dead. And if Redhill was the son, even the grandson of some old war criminal, what would that prove? Nazism was not an inheritable gene. On the other hand, what must it have been like to grow up in one of those colonies where they all married each other to preserve both the purity of the *herrenvolk* and the safety of the group? What did they talk about late at night after the birthday or wedding anniversary party, sitting around with the final glass of *schnapps* in their hand? The good old days? When one of the old men died did the survivors reminisce about the times they had when they were young men – where? Parents had to justify themselves to their children. Did they recall their roles with pride? There were ways, thought Borash, to inherit acquired characteristics, unscientific but no less predictable ways than genital contact. Acquired characteristics could be inherited as ideas, passed on like family heirlooms from generation to generation, treasured, cherished, valued, their worth never questioned. Maybe Redhill – or Rotberg – had inherited his share of ideas just as he, Borash, had inherited his. And if he had never questioned their truth and validity might it not have been the same with Redhill-Rotberg. Maybe that accounted for the Professor's groundless hostility – even hatred – for the way he never lost a chance to stress that he, Redhill, was superior and had the power. It would also account for the Professor's ruthlessness.

How stupid he was becoming, Borash thought. Weren't all the scientists he had ever worked with ruthless when they felt they were on the track of an important discovery, something that might bring them fame, money, perhaps a Nobel prize? And were they not even more unpleasant and ruthless when their ideas stubbornly refused to flower, when theory obstinately remained unproven? No. No matter what Rotberg-Redhill's background was, he behaved no differently from all the other crazy scientists he had worked with. Maybe some of that craziness had worked off on him. After all, wasn't he a scientist too? That was a good second in biology he had got at

Birmingham. And, speaking as a scientist, thinking the thing out scientifically, wasn't it possible that the little Nazi bastard hated him simply because he was not very likeable. Would a democrat or a liberal like him more? Unlikely. Did anyone like him, much less love him? But wouldn't it be wonderful if he could find just one person who would. Be honest, Borash, he told himself. You don't mean person, you mean woman. One woman. A fat chance. Especially now, hairless as a shelled egg.

His thoughts were broken by the shrilling of the libidogram. At it again, he thought. Would they never stop?

Penny and HM didn't know about the bell but it would not have made much difference if they had. They had grown used to the idea that they were overlooked and overheard most of the time and no longer even bothered to cover their nakedness as they walked between bedroom and bathroom. Even HM no longer minded now.

Penny snuggled up against him under the single sheet that was all they needed as cover in that always warm, always insulated room. It would be nice to get out, she thought but, at the same time, there were worse ways of passing a week or two. That was all it was going to be. Richard had told her so and she liked the plump little Minister and thought that, within the limits allowed by his official position, he was on their side. She had seen him on one of her exercise outings. She and HM were allowed out every day for an hour or two but always separately, the Professor having rightly reasoned that one would not try to escape without the other. She had been walking with Borash when they had bumped into the Minister in what seemed to be an accidental meeting though she would not have been surprised to learn that it was engineered. Bendigo had touched her cheek gently and asked if they were being treated all right. He seemed relieved when she told him that neither she nor HM had much to complain of except, of course, the lack of freedom.

'It will only be a week or two,' he had said, 'a month at the outside. I know it's no consolation but the rats are getting worse and the shortages are getting worse and I can't think of anything that's getting better and on the whole I envy you.' Then he added wistfully, 'At least I envy your friend.' With that he had walked away and Borash had said: 'For a politician he seems almost human.' This was very odd because it made her think that, for a scientist, Borash was almost human.

She was thinking about the evening she had met both HM and Bendigo for the first time, the casual remark by HM that had started off the whole business. Sleepily, she said: 'You never told me what happened after you left us that day.'

'What day?' mumbled HM.

'After that meal in the Bulgarian restaurant. With Harvey Hall.'

'Oh that. Nothing much.'

'But how did they find you? Where did you go?'

'There weren't many places,' said HM. 'All I knew was that whatever was going to happen it couldn't be worse than the kind of thing Hall was talking about. So I just left. I had no idea where I was going. I couldn't go home because I was sure they'd have found out where I lived and would be watching it. I was equally sure they'd be watching Freedom's place. There was nowhere else I knew – except Dora's.'

'You went back there!' gasped Penny incredulously.

'I thought it would be the one place the police wouldn't be watching,' said HM. 'And I was right.'

'Dora never told me,' said Penny. 'I saw quite a lot of her afterwards. It was through her I got my pass to this place.'

'I know,' said HM, though Penny was not quite sure

whether he meant that he knew that Dora had not told her, that she had spent a lot of time with Dora or that she had got her pass from Dora. 'Dora was in and didn't seem surprised to see me when she opened the door.'

'But what did she say?'

'That she was sorry this had happened but that it had nothing to do with her. She also said that she still retained enough commitment to the idea of personal freedom that she would not be a party to anything which threatened it for any innocent person, no matter what the political repercussions were or what effect it would have on her career. She would think of some way to get me away, she said, or, if not, try to get the whole thing called off. In any case I was safe there for a while.'

'So what happened?'

'She said she had an appointment and told me to make myself at home until she got back. Then she left and ten minutes later the police came.'

'You could have been seen going in.'

'They didn't have to break the door down. I was in the bath when they walked in. I heard the key in the lock. I thought it was Dora coming back. They hauled me out of the bath and were very careful not to leave a mess. I was given time to dry and dress and I saw one policeman tidying up the bathroom as we left. I bet by the time she got back there was no trace of my ever having been there. She could have dreamt it.'

'She is a Cabinet Minister,' said Penny. 'The police may have a key to her flat; naturally they wouldn't want to leave a mess. I bet she's moving heaven and earth to get us out of here.'

'Maybe.'

'You mean,' said Clementina, horror in her voice, 'that they are making them breed? That's disgusting.'

'They're not actually forcing them to have intercourse,'

said Dora. 'They don't have to. All they will do is to take Penny's pills away.'

'If they did that to me,' said Clementina, 'I just wouldn't do it; that's all. There are alternatives.'

'She won't know. They'll take the pills away and put others in their place,' said Dora. 'They'll look the same but they'll be harmless – I mean they won't work.'

'That's diabolical,' whistled Freedom.'

'The bastards,' said Clementina. 'Why are you telling us all this? It's your lousy government that's doing it.'

'I hope,' said Dora with simple dignity, 'that I haven't completely lost my commitment to personal freedom. And what's more Clem I'm hurt that you should think that I have sold out to this extent.'

'Of course you've sold out,' snapped Clementina. 'Just like Bendigo and all the others. There was a time when I thought that if only people like you could get into office everything would be changed, that for once there'd be no betrayal.'

'There are limits Clem. Collective Cabinet responsibility is a powerful weapon against protest – '

'There are no limits Dora, not if you really meant what you used to say. Society must be changed you said, a better, saner world. Now you've sold out as well – you're only concerned with your career, with holding on to power. Haven't I risked my career enough? You can't imagine the number of roles I've lost because some fool can't distinguish between the actress and the politician. And the number of roles I've turned down because I can't either. But what have you done since the PM picked you off the back benches to keep you quiet? Where would you be if we took to the streets again like we should to save HM and Penny and protest against the thousand other things that are wrong in this crummy society that you're holding together with sticking plaster? Would you be marching with us or would you be behind the troops, the first to order them to fire the IG cannisters?'

Freedom's head swivelled to Dora in anticipation of her reply. It was not disappointed. She could return rhetoric with a steady forehand drive that would send her opponent running backwards to the baseline.

'Do you think all the virtue is on your side Clementina? Do you think it easy to compromise? To give way on a hundred little matters in order to save one big one, to sacrifice a thousand yards of ground in order to stand at one major pass? Who has done the most for the causes we believe in – you with your political demands for instant change in a society that is suspicious of any change at all and rejects all sudden shifts of direction, or I with the long hours spent working out something with my officials and then fighting for it to the point of exhaustion in Cabinet against the recommendations of the Treasury ministers – and winning? It is only by gritting my teeth and hanging on to my job that I've been able to serve the causes we have always believed in. It would have been easier many times to pack it in. There are plenty of lucrative jobs for ex-Ministers of Culture, especially those who resign on a point of principle.'

Exhausted, she sat down on Freedom's sofa. Freedom looked admiringly at her, gave Clementina his camera and posed next to Dora. Then he gave Dora the camera and posed next to Clementina. It was his way of indicating that he thought it was a draw.

'None of this solves the problem of getting them to release HM and Penny,' said Clementina, her voice more conciliatory than it had been. 'God, if we could only take to the streets again! There are thousands just aching to get out there and show those bastards what we think of them. They'd only have to be told about the way HM and Penny are being treated and there'd be a roar of protest that would make Downing Street shake.'

‘Where are they being kept?’ asked Freedom.

‘At the Government research station,’ said Dora.

‘Yes, but where?’

Dora hesitated and then said, ‘A place called Mountfitchet.’

Freedom rolled it round his tongue: ‘The Mountfitchet Two,’ he said, adding, ‘That’s no fucking good, is it. Where’s it near?’

‘It’s between Saffron Walden – ’ Freedom groaned – ‘and Chelmsford.’

He brightened up. ‘The Chelmsford Two,’ he said, ‘that’s better. Free the Chelmsford Two!’

‘Right on,’ cheered Clementina, then remembered. ‘What’s the use,’ she said. ‘The moment we get a crowd together in Trafalgar Square they’ll use the IGs and we’ll be standing like statues in the rain for the next three hours – with pigeons on our heads.’

‘I wouldn’t be so sure,’ said Dora. It took a second or so for Clementina to realize what she had said.

‘What do you mean?’

‘Just that there are no incapacitating gases any more. We had a report the other day that they had discovered that no matter how well they are stored they have an inbuilt instability that makes them harmless in ten years. It must be twelve years since we last used them and we closed the plant that made them simply because there was no longer any call for the stuff and we had plenty stockpiled. But it’s all harmless now. You can fetch ’em out on the streets if you like, just like the old days. It’ll be all the more effective for not having been done for so many years. Fetch ’em out Clem. Mob Downing Street and Parliament. Bring out the masses. Maybe there’s more life in the old radical than you thought.’

Clementina clasped a blissful Dora in her arms.

‘Oh Dora, I’m so sorry. I was wrong. You’re the same old Dora. We’ll do it. Won’t we Freedom, we’ll do it.’

She disengaged herself from Dora and flung her arms open wide. 'Free the Chelmsford Two,' she cried. 'Fight the Whitehall Fascists!'

She faced Freedom and rapped out an order: 'Leaflets, pamphlets, placards, posters.'

She went to the door and shouted: 'We're taking to the streets again; we're marching against fascism again; we're demonstrating for freedom again; we are on the march again!' But the Total Art Environment was empty. However, her passionate cries were heard by a street sweeper outside who went to the nearest telephone box and reported in.

The demo was a great success. 20,000 people, mostly young, crammed into Trafalgar Square and heard some rousing speeches. Among those on the rostrum were a trade union leader, two Members of Parliament, a Bishop and Clementina herself. All stressed the need for preserving the liberty of the individual at all costs. Cases of a similar nature in South Africa and various South American republics were cited, evidence of the Government's approval of crimes against the individual being drawn from their support of these reactionary regimes. A request smuggled out of a Soviet labour camp by a detainee who requested an invitation to speak at the rally was turned down by the ad hoc organizing committee on the grounds that there was no possible way of the detainee getting to Trafalgar Square on time. He was told, however, that the event would undoubtedly be reported on the BBC World Service so he would be able to hear what happened.

The Government had thoroughly prepared for the occasion. A week before the first question about HM and Penny was tabled in the House of Commons, the description of the Mountfitchet establishment was changed from research station to isolation clinic. They had then maintained in the House, in Ministerial interviews with the media and in exclusive leaks to lobby correspondents that HM and Penny were suffering from an unknown but highly contagious condition and were being held in isolation, both for their own sakes and the safety of the general public. They would be released as soon as the condition had run its course – whatever that may be – and it was considered safe to let them loose.

A similar case was convincingly argued by the Attorney-General when lawyers acting for Clementina issued a writ of habeas corpus. The judge ruled that just as he would not require the authorities to produce a body suffering from some such contagious disease as lassa fever because of the danger of infecting the public, to say nothing of the court, he was equally powerless in the face of this unknown condition which clearly required prolonged medical investigation. He would therefore not refuse the writ of habeas corpus but would adjourn the hearing to a date to be set after consultations with the appropriate government department.

When pressed, the government disclosed that Dr Henry Redhill was in charge of the team of investigative scientists and a gifted reporter who remembered a story he had written not twelve months previously asked if this Dr Redhill was not the same man who had been trying to find a solution to the rat problem. That was so, he was told, but the brilliant doctor had been put in charge of this new development and would return to the rat problem as soon as HM and Penny had been discharged. No doubt this would be quite soon.

None of this was believed by the thousands who gathered in Trafalgar Square and preferred the ad hoc committee's version of events which, roughly, was that the whole set-up was a conspiracy between the reactionary government and a lickspittle fascist press. This, of course, was largely true, though there was probably more manipulation involved than the ad hoc committee gave the government credit for. Just how much was not immediately apparent.

Clementina and her ad hoc committee were more than a little surprised when the forces of law and order present at the mass meeting made no effort to prevent them marching down Whitehall to deliver a petition to 10 Downing Street. They attributed this laxness to inexperience on the part of the police, all the senior officers involved in the earlier demonstrations having retired, being by now well established in their second careers.

But not as surprised as she was ten minutes later when, shortly before she froze in angry stillness, she realized that the air was thick with incapacitating gases. She, Freedom, the trade union leader, the two MPs, the Bishop and many others stood there for three hours, most of which she spent planning acts of vengeance on Dora and speculating why the Minister had gone to such lengths to deceive her. She did not know that behind her police and army barricades had been set up and were netting the several thousand young people who, without gas masks, were wandering through the IG clouds puzzled as to why everything had come to a sudden stop. They were taken off to some very comfortable camps.

Shortly afterwards they were joined by many thousands more as a result of Borash discovering that both HM and Penny possessed an extra chromosome which Professor Redhill called the 'R' (for Redhill) chromosome. This could be located very easily during the course of any ordinary blood test and the Government issued an order that doctors must communicate its presence to the authorities, just as if it were whooping cough or German measles.

There was some unrest among the families but no more mass demonstrations and the Prime Minister said that he would shortly make an announcement that would fill his listeners with joy at the prospect of a wonderful revival in the fortunes of this grand old country of ours.

And so he did. He announced that evolution had taken a giant stride forward and that, in its wisdom, it had selected members of this favoured nation for its blessing. The future held unbounded promise if only this new development was handled with wisdom and foresight, that is, by the Government. All the immunees were to be brought to a mass rally in Hyde Park where he would address them himself. It would be televised not only to the nation but to the whole wide envious world outside.

When the day came every member of the Cabinet, two archbishops, Dr Redhill and the top disc jockey of the day were all seated on the platform surrounded by a huge crowd of young people, their faces reflecting curiosity and a little fear. In the distance, around the perimeter of the park, could be glimpsed the transports that had brought them there and a thin sprinkling of khaki and blue uniforms.

'What's stopping them just getting up and going home?' whispered Dora to Bendigo. 'The Army and the Police could never prevent them.'

'What stops them,' said Bendigo, 'is that they want to be together. They've been told that they're different, that they are special, that they have been segregated from the rest of the population because they are a new order of human beings. They're frightened and bewildered and they need the comfort of others who are feeling the same. You don't need barbed wire or soldiers to keep this lot together. They have formed their own tribe. All they need is some kind of recognition mark; as things are the only way they know each other is because they are together. If they split up they would not be able to recognize another immunee and would be intolerably lonely. They will not split up – and there will be no pressure from them for freedom – until they learn to create an identification mark for themselves. Until they do that they cannot leave the safety of the group.'

In the distance a pop band spluttered to a stop and the disc jockey's voice boomed over the park.

'Thank you, thank you. That was that great new group Horseshit, brought here especially today to entertain you kids. Weren't they great? So give them a big hand.'

A thin sputter of applause rippled through the overwhelming indifference of the crowd.

'Thank you, thank you kids,' the disc jockey oozed. 'I'm sure Horseshit is going to go a long way. And now, and now for the moment you've all been waiting for, the reason you were brought here today, to this fantastic gig, the greatest event even this historic old Park has seen. So here it is, ladies and gentlemen, the man you elected as your leader all those years ago, a big hand for your Prime Minister.'

'I'll give you five to one he doesn't get as much applause as Horseshit,' whispered Dora to Bendigo.

'Not taken,' he said. His judgement was immediately proved right.

'Thank you,' said the Prime Minister, 'thank you Steve for that wonderful introduction. Ladies and gentlemen, young people, may I say, the future of Britain. By now most of you will have realized what great effort the Government has put into securing your future and the future of this great old country of ours. Some of you, I dare say, do not fully appreciate our methods. I can understand that. To have been dragooned into camps – no matter how comfortable, even, I dare say, luxurious by some standards – is not something that free-born Britons like yourselves take to kindly. But you have my word for it – you *are* free, more free now and in the future than anyone has ever been in the past. You will have the kind of freedom that old campaigners like myself and my colleagues here, all of them known to you as staunch champions of liberty, could only dream of. For why? Let me tell you. You are freer than anyone has ever been before because you are very special people, unlike anyone who has ever lived before. You yourselves may not have fully realized this, but all of you, without exception, have passed a test which marks you out as exceptional human beings. You are the immunees, immune, that is, from the effects of the polluted atmosphere we have inherited from our short-sighed predecessors. You have evolved into a new kind of human being as far removed from your ancestors, from us, as we are from prehistoric man. The great march of evolution has taken a giant step forward for mankind in general, for Britain in particular.

'It is the government's duty – and I can say without fear of contradiction that this government has never shirked its duty, no matter how unpopular – or even popular – that duty might be – to make special provision for such special cases. For the future of this great nation of ours lies with you, the new breed of Briton. The old order goeth; the new order is here. In the main you represent what has been called the counter-culture. Well, I can say to you that as from today the counter-culture prevails. Your libertarian philosophy has triumphed. Now it is not our intention to force anyone to practise a way of life that is repugnant to them and I am sure it would be equally repugnant to you if we tried to do so. That means that for a time the old ways will have to continue alongside the new ways. And I did say alongside. Not together, not all mixed up. That way lies only chaos and confusion. But in time the old ways will die out naturally and you will be left, inheritors of the world, masters of all you survey.

'For the most important task facing us all today – immunees and those of us who are going to be replaced by your vibrant new genes – is to prevent dilution of those very special qualities that have brought you here today. To that end, special centres have been built where you will have every facility to pursue a life of meaningful pleasure. Work is already proceeding to turn these camps – centres – into model towns where your every need will be provided by a grateful nation. Indeed, in order to prevent infiltration by others who, sadly, are not equipped to share your way of life, they will, for the time, being, be specially guarded by men whose duty will be to look after your interests.

'We have reached a turning point in the history of our people, indeed, in the history of the world, and we ignore it at our peril. Do not think we are trying to impose any of our old, outmoded ideas on you. We have taken careful note of all the demands expressed throughout the years in your underground newspapers, the literature of protest, the lyrics of your music. Henceforth your communities will be run on the lines you have always demanded. There will be no more marriage! The bourgeois institution has been abolished. There will be no more money, at least not in your special towns; to each according to his needs, from each according to his inclinations. We outside will gladly undertake the labour that is needed to protect you from the distractions and pressures of what has, up till now, been known as day-to-day living but which many young people have truly categorized as a rat race in which they wished to play no part. In the past they have been called "drop-outs". From today they are "drop-ins". For them, for you all, there will be the opportunity to develop the artistic talents which you have always claimed, quite rightly, to lie within each and every one of us. For my generation these talents have been stunted by the need to earn our daily bread; to you there will be no such inhibitor of growth. All will be equal. We will not distinguish, I promise you, between the great talent and the small talent – the luck of inherited gifts will play no role in your young lives as the luck of inherited fortune with all its injustice and inequality has played in ours. Competition for greater reward will not exist because it will not be necessary. Greed, which has disfigured every civilization, every life-style yet created by man, will be unknown in your communes. Possessions will be shared; no man shall have more than his brother, no woman more than her sister. The children? I hear you ask. Special care will be taken of the children. They are our future. It is they who will inherit the earth and all its riches, giving this nation the place it has earned in the forefront of civilization. The future is assured; the future is yours. Thank you.'

The thin splutter of applause was magnified by the loudspeakers and bolstered by a tape recording of a television quiz show audience. The disc jockey bounced back to the microphone, whipped the head off the stand and, swinging his head from side to side, the microphone never more than an inch from his teeth, said: 'Horseshit will be back in just a few minutes folks. But before then a few words from the Bishop of Kensington.'

In full regalia, the Bishop emerged from behind the stand took the microphone from the disc jockey, made the sign of blessing the crowd and with great emotion, intoned: 'Go forth and multiply.'

Bendigo had moved off and the Prime Minister sat down in his place next to Dora. 'If that doesn't put up the birth-rate,' he said, 'I don't know what will. They'll have nothing to do all day but copulate. And the one thing they won't get is the pill. I tell you something else, Dora, it solves the unemployment problem at a stroke.'

'We'll have to be careful about the pill, Prime Minister. I expect the soldiers will smuggle it in. We'll have to keep a close eye on them.'

'I don't think there's much danger there, Dora,' said

the PM. 'Don't forget, the immunees will have no money, nothing to pay the soldiers with. Oh it will work all right, Dora, thanks to you. It was a brilliant idea to get them on the streets again. You know, I've been thinking for some time of making a few changes. I'm not entirely happy with the way some of our colleagues are coping with their departments. Some of them have gone quite stale, no enthusiasm.'

'Thank you Prime Minister,' said Dora. She wondered where Bendigo had got to. It was very foolish to leave before the Prime Minister.

Chapter 8

'If,' said HM, 'we're as special as they say we are why aren't we clever enough to get out of here?'

'Maybe we are just superior physical specimens, like gorillas in a zoo. They can't get out either,' said Penny.

They were sitting facing each other in armchairs. They had long since decided to ignore the observation and the eavesdropping, though when they had anything intimate or important to say to each other they would either use a notepad or the shower, depending on the circumstances. They had taken a shower half an hour before when they had decided what their next move would be.

Penny added: 'I suppose we'll just have to wait here till they've finished with us. Thank God for Borash.'

'Yes,' said HM, 'I like Borash. If anyone should be trying to get away from this place it's him. He suffers far more than we do.'

'He's a truly dedicated man, HM. You can see how he sacrifices himself in the cause of science. It's strange, though, the way he keeps having these accidents while the Professor is unharmed. I sometimes think – no, it couldn't be, I must be wrong . . . '

'What?'

'Well, you know how scientists hate to share the credit for a discovery. And you know it was Borash who identified the R gene – '

' – shouldn't it have been the B gene?' asked HM.

'Maybe the Professor is deliberately . . . '

'No, surely Borash is too clever for that. Besides, they're both Jews aren't they and you know how Jews stick together.'

'I don't suppose all Jews always stick together. I expect some Jews don't like some other Jews. Poor Borash. And such an attractive man too. Even without his hair, his teeth and – '

Borash entered the room which was in one of its periodic clean air cycles. He was on crutches, his right leg hanging loose, swinging uselessly, as he levered himself across the floor.

'Hello Borash,' said HM, 'we were just talking about you.'

'It's not fair,' said Borash. 'You knew I was listening. What do you have to say things like that for?'

'Listening? We thought you just looked and had us wired up for blood pressure and things like that. We didn't know you listened as well.'

'Listening,' echoed Penny. 'The Professor told us he no longer used the microphones. Do you mean you heard all those nice things I was saying about you Borash? What's your Christian name anyway – we can't keep on calling you Borash.'

'Christian name? That's a joke.'

'Come on Borash, what is it?'

'Moses.'

'That's a very nice name,' said Penny, 'though I admit it's not very Christian.'

'Enough of that,' said Borash. 'I only came in to adjust your metabolic beam. We're getting a reading that makes no sense at all. It's all right, you don't have to do anything, it's in the wall.'

He unlocked a concealed panel revealing a set of dials. He adjusted one and then slammed the panel shut.

'Don't get any ideas about those instruments,' he said. 'If you could do anything to them – and you can't – it will only mean that you have to stay here longer.'

'How much longer will we have to stay anyway?' asked Penny. 'Why do you need us at all? You've got all the other immunees at Bletchley to work on.'

'There's no point on selecting a couple and starting all over again,' said Borash. 'The Professor hasn't finished his tests yet.'

'Experiments you mean, Moses, don't you. Experiments, not tests,' challenged Penny.

'Tests,' corrected Borash firmly. 'If they'd been experiments you would have suffered pain and I wouldn't have had anything to do with that. Rats yes, human beings no. All that's happening to you is things like chromosome counts, cell analysis, genetic calibration, metabolic monitoring, things like that.'

'But why can't you just take the samples you need and let us go?' asked HM.

'Because we don't know when we will need more. We're working through a whole series of experi – tests – and we don't know what the answers are until we find them. We hardly even know the questions. No one's ever had a human evolutionary mechanism to work on before.'

'But I thought it went on all the time. Evolution, I mean,' said Penny. 'Look at your people; they've evolved differently from everyone else haven't they?'

'Jews you mean? Not physically at any rate. Though there are some genetic differences that make us more prone to some diseases and less prone to others.'

'But everyone knows you're cleverer than everyone else. And better scientists and better musicians. Isn't that evolution?'

'And better at frauds and fiddles too. No, that's not real evolution though there's perhaps a crude element of natural selection involved. If you took any identifiable group of people and regularly attacked them for a couple of thousand years you would find that the slow-witted and the dull-minded were the last to realize what was about to happen and the first to find themselves at the sharp end of a sword, or a gun, or an inquisitor's rack. The clever ones – and the cunning ones – the ones who had the wit to acquire a portable skill such as fiddle-playing or diamond cutting or merely the ability to understand and manipulate market forces, were not only the first to get away but had the means to enable them to flourish in their new environment.

'Of course, as technology improved, the big wholesale murderers reaped the benefits of progress and the clever and the wise went into the ovens alongside the dunces. But the process had been so haphazard for so many centuries that the survival factors were naturally prominent among the Jews who escaped the camps. Just let the Jews alone for a couple of centuries and you'll find as large a measure of stupidity among them as in any other population. It has already happened in Israel and it's beginning to happen in Jewish communities in the West as well.'

HM said: 'But to a large extent you've kept your racial exclusivity more than anyone else. If there are genetic changes, even small ones as you say, surely it would be easy to isolate them?'

'Racial purity! You must be joking. Obviously you know nothing about Jewish history. There are Indian Jews who look like Hindus, Sephardi Jews who left Spain 500 years ago and are still proud of their Spanish appearance, Arab Jews who could walk the streets of Tripoli without being noticed and probably do and Ethiopian Jews as black as any Rastafarian. You think you know what a Jew looks like? Go to Poland where most of the Jews you have seen originated and you will find that they all look Jewish, though there are very few Jews living there these days. It's not for nothing that the one essential qualification for being a Jew is to have a Jewish mother. Not when you have been at the mercy of Roman soldiers, Arab and Turkish slavers or raided by Cossacks every Easter for 1,000 years or more. Every minority inhabits an occupied country. There's not one Jewish family from Eastern Europe which does not have a story about an aunt who was raped in a pogrom. But no one has a cousin who isn't 100 per cent Jewish. The more you look at it, the more it seems likely that some of the greatest antisemites in Europe fathered some of the most troublesome Jews.'

'But in that case,' said HM, 'how does heredity come into it? What about all those Cossack genes? It looks as if environment is the totally deciding factor.'

'There's nothing wrong with the Cossack genes once they're inside the right body,' said Borash. 'They probably contain a great deal of energy and power. All the Jewish environment does is to channel that energy into a different direction from the one it would have taken in a Cossack environment.'

'All the same,' said HM, 'I would have thought that with your history, you and Professor Redhill would be the last to lock up people in order to conduct experiments on them.'

'I don't know why you should think that,' said Borash, testily. 'I suppose that theoretically you are entitled to expect a higher standard of morality from a very religious Jew, just as you would expect one from a very religious Christian for both lay down rules about righteous behaviour. But I am a non-believer and you have no right to expect a greater sense of morality from a Jewish non-believer than I have from a Christian non-believer,'

'But if you cannot define a Jew by race,' said Penny, 'and you can't define him by his beliefs, how is it that you still consider yourself to be a Jew?'

'A Jew is defined by others,' said Borash. 'You think of me as a Jew, therefore I am a Jew. If you asked me to describe myself I would answer according to the circumstances. If I'm abroad I'm British, if I'm in Scotland, I'm English. I am middle-aged, a theatregoer, a husband, a father, a scientist – all depending on who is asking the question. You see me only as a Jew or at least you see my Jewishness as the most significant thing about me. I see it as being of secondary importance for most of the time; it becomes of primary importance only when someone wants to hit me for it, or, in more extreme circumstances, kill me.

'But you and a great many of my liberal-minded acquaintances go out of their way to make sure that we discuss only the one small but important fraction of me that is Jewish, simply so that they can demonstrate that they do not look upon it as a forbidden or even a difficult subject. I am a living example of their tolerance, though even that distinction is being taken away from me by blacks. As for religion, hasn't the Jew the same right as any Christian to be an atheist?'

'And Professor Redhill?'

'Like most English people – ' began Borash.

'My parents were American,' interrupted Penny.

'You have the same cultural references – you make the mistake of thinking that any scientist with a foreign accent or name is a Jew. The fact is that Professor Redhill is of German origin and was born in Paraguay. Maybe his grandfather, like mine, was at Auschwitz.'

'So he is a Jew then,' said HM.

'No, my grandfather was an inmate and was killed there; his would have been a guard. But I don't doubt he is as much a victim of his family's myths about the past as I am of mine. Which is not to say that all myths are equal.'

'Is he listening to us now?' asked Penny.

'No, he's been called to a conference in London. The Prime Minister sent for him this morning. And I've turned off the recorder.'

'Why did you do that?' asked HM.

'I didn't know what else you were going to say about me and I didn't want to be compromised by your praise.

I do not think it is genuine, especially your talk about my physical attractiveness.'

The telephone rang in the outer room. Borash struggled painfully through the open airlock door and they heard him answer. From his replies it was clear that it was the Professor at the other end. When he put the telephone down he came straight back.

Without preliminary he said: 'I no longer wish to be associated with this scientific investigation.'

'Why?' asked HM.

'Because Professor Redhill is planning to take the tests one stage further,' said Borash. 'He has just received the Prime Minister's permission. He's so excited he wanted me to prepare you. He's on his way back.'

'What is he going to do?'

'He has a theory that genetic change originates in the brain and that if the area can be located and the mechanism understood then we can assume responsibility for our own evolution.'

'That sounds fantastic,' said Penny, 'but is it feasible?'

'It is unlikely, but I couldn't rule it out altogether,' said Borash.

'In that case why don't you want to carry on with the tests?' asked HM.

'Because we shall have to start removing sections of your brain. Professor Redhill was reluctant to do this at first but now that there is a plentiful supply of immunees at Bletchley he feels he can take the risk.'

'He can take the risk!' shrieked Penny.

'I thought experiments of this kind were illegal,' said HM.

'So they are,' said Borash, 'but the Prime Minister and other members of the Cabinet are apparently very interested and once that happens illegality becomes a mere technical problem. If Professor Redhill is right they look forward to him being able to stimulate the changes that will make them immunees also. Ms Dodd, the new Minister of Science, is especially keen.'

Penny started to cry. 'They can't start cutting up our brains,' she said.

'Don't cry,' said Borash. 'They won't do it.'

'Does that mean you'll help us to escape?' asked HM.

'It's quite simple if you want to.'

'How do we get past the guards? What about the guns?'

'The guards are to prevent people getting in, not you getting out, though it helps if you think they are. In fact, they have strict instructions that on no account must you be hurt, even slightly. Not even the slightest tap with a truncheon. At least not on the head.'

Penny moaned.

'But they have stopped us whenever we've got too near the main gate,' said HM.

'And one once pointed a gun at me,' said Penny.

'If he had used it he would have been shot himself,' said Borash. 'No, all they can do is to seize you, as gently as possible, and bring you back and lock you in.'

'Even so, we're no match for them,' said Penny. 'HM is not exactly a heavyweight.'

'Just behind that door,' said Borash, 'there are two canisters of the stuff we were pouring into this room all last week – not that it did you any harm. But it's deadly to anyone else, including me. All you have to do is to point the nozzle at anyone who stands in your way and give them a whiff or two if they don't move pretty sharpish. But they'll move all right; they know what it can do to them. They remember me as I used to be.'

'But they have gas-masks.'

'They leave them in the next room; it's the only place they ever expect to use them. Certainly not out in the open.'

'So we can just walk out of here and no one can stop us?'

'That's right. Just choose a calm day when there's not much wind.'

'Won't you get into trouble?' asked Penny.

'I reckon I've got another month or six weeks to live,' said Borash unemotionally. 'So what can they do? The canisters are behind the door; the door is open; there's not much of a wind so you might as well go now.'

Penny kissed him. 'Moses, oh Moses,' was all she could say.

Borash showed no reaction.

As he was leaving the room HM stopped and turned round.

'What are you going to do about the Professor, Moses?'

'Do?' Borash considered. It was as if the thought had not even entered his head before. 'What is there to do? I cannot hold him responsible for the deeds of his grandfather; after all, one must set better standards than God in these matters. And I am not at all sure that he has deliberately engineered the things that have happened to me. And if he has, that same God whom I do not believe in has issued firm instructions that vengeance is his so I can do nothing there. You see, like most Jews, I only reject those aspects of God of which I disapprove; where God's nature coincides with my beliefs I don't quarrel with him.'

'You're a good man, Moses,' said Penny. 'I've never met anyone with less malice.'

Borash laughed. 'I wouldn't be so sure,' he said. 'How do you think Professor Rotberg – '

'Professor who?' cut in HM.

'Rotberg, Redhill, what's the difference? How do you think he'll feel when he finds the cage empty. You are his road to glory and he's going to be frantic.'

'He'll take it out on you, won't he?' said Penny.

'I suppose so. In fact I hope so. Where's the fun if he doesn't. Especially when he finds that George is missing too.'

'George?'

'Our prize rat out there. I'm going to let him out as well. He's earned it. If anything, he's had more to put up with than you . . . For one thing he's had no sex life for a year. That's very tough on a rat.'

'It's not so easy on a human either,' said HM.

When they were outside the gates and out of sight, Penny said: 'Where can we go? They'll be watching Freedom and Clem and we haven't any money.'

'I've been thinking about that,' said HM. 'It seems to me that the only place we can go is Bletchley and join up with the others.'

'It'll be nice to be with our own kind,' said Penny. 'With people who won't think of us as a couple of freaks. Though it will still mean being cooped up like prisoners.'

'At least it's bigger,' said HM. 'Not just one small room. From what we saw on television it looked like a small town. People seemed happy enough.'

'They look happy on the commercials, too,' said Penny. 'Happy and mad. I thought they had that same crazy look as though they were about to start shrieking with delight over something that ordinary people don't notice, or at least don't get excited about, like the difference between two tins of furniture polish or two bars of chocolate.'

'Does that make them mad?'

'Sure it does. It's as if they only believed lies, no matter how far-fetched or how ridiculous they were and would never believe the truth, no matter how sensible it sounded. That's being mad in exactly the same way as people who think they are being controlled by radio signals sent from outer space while they are unable to believe someone a yard away who says it isn't so.'

'They can't all be like that at Bletchley; they're ordinary people just like us. We've all undergone some genetic change that no one quite understands yet, but it's only happened to our bodies, our minds are unaffected and our behaviour hasn't changed. Until they put us to the test no one had the slightest inkling that we were in any way different. If they didn't like it at Bletchley all they would have to do would be to walk out and mingle with the rest of the people. They'd never be found again, not unless they screened the whole population.'

'I expect they're guarded,' said Penny.

'They didn't show that on television.'

'They wouldn't would they?'

'So what do you suggest then?'

'Nothing. There's not much choice is there? We either make our way to Bletchley or we go back to our room. There's nowhere else.'

George burrowed deeply into the debris at the bottom of the ditch and lay low until nightfall. Once it was dark he would set off in search of his own kind. He trembled with anticipations of joy. He had never felt stronger or fitter. He would, he thought, fuck every female rat within reach and fight any fucker who tried to stop him. Though he did not realize it – not then at least – George had just crossed the threshold of another stage of evolution. He was the first rat ever to plan ahead.

Chapter 9

'It's very difficult,' said Dora. 'When Professor Redhill's work was sabotaged by that demented assistant of his, months of work went down the drain.'

'While the rats came up it,' snapped the Prime Minister. 'It's no use Dora, you've had the Ministry for six months now and we seem no nearer a solution.'

'But Prime Minister,' protested Dora, 'I cannot work miracles. Research into the rat immunity problem has been going on for far longer than that without producing anything of a practical nature.'

'That,' said the Prime Minister, 'is precisely why I put you in charge. I expected big things from you Dora – but the rats still prosper, more than ever, it seems. For that matter, we don't seem to be getting any further with the human immunee programme either. Unlike the rats they're not having babies.'

'But Prime Minister, it's only six months since we opened the Bletchley Camp. There's never been any suggestion of an evolutionary change in the human gestation period.'

'You know as well as I do that that's not the point – most of them are not even pregnant.'

'Yes,' said Dora, 'and I had a hand-picked team of my people infiltrated into Bletchley. I received their report this morning.'

'They've found out, I suppose, that the new fashion is celibacy among the young,' said the Prime Minister in his most sarcastic fashion.

'As it so happens,' said Dora, 'that is what a small number practice, but,' she added hastily, 'it is too small to have any statistical significance. No, it seems there is a genuine resistance to our expectations of fecundity while, being young, there is no tendency to forgo the pleasures of sex.'

'They're getting contraceptives from somewhere then?'

'A few are being smuggled in. Young soldiers can be bribed easily by young girls without any money changing hands. No, the resistance to impregnation is manifested in a number of ways, most of them traditional. First of all there is oral sex which is taking place on a scale larger than at any time since the mid-sixties when oral gratification was discovered. You are, I suppose, familiar with the work carried out by Tustin and Westby on the correlation of cigarette renunciation with the reduction in lung cancer and oral gratification with the increase in throat cancer? Yes, I thought you would be. Anyway, that is one method. The other, of course, is more time-honoured and I refer, of course, to homosexuality. But even here I must confess to have been shocked by a perversion which I gather is completely new to those who make a specialist study of such matters. It seems that mixed parties are being held in which all the stimulation comes from interplay of a heterosexual nature, while all the consequences of arousal are expended in a homosexual situation. Needless to say, Prime Minister, no true homosexual would ever lend herself – or even himself – to such indecent practices and those fellow homosexuals with whom I have discussed this new and disgusting trend have been as horrified as I was.'

'But you were only given the report this morning,' observed the Prime Minister. 'How could you have discussed it with – er – fellow homosexuals?'

'I discussed it,' said Dora, 'with members of the team of investigators who went into the camp. I resent any suggestion that I may have in any way contravened the Official Secrets Act.'

'I wouldn't dream of making any such suggestion,' the Prime Minister said hastily. 'I have never had any scintilla of doubt about your loyalty.'

Good, thought Dora, I've got the old prick on the defensive at last.

'What does concern me, however,' the Prime Minister continued, 'is that while we may have our problems at Bletchley they are of a long term nature while the more pressing, the more immediate and the more important, at least when looked at from an electoral point of view, is the business of the rats. Their incursions are becoming more and more frequent and more and more flagrant. There were two coupling in my kitchen this morning and the male rat was so aggressive when approached that my cook was frightened to go near. When he'd finished he just strolled to the cellar door and squeezed underneath it. Even the leg of chicken he'd picked up on the way gave him no problems. He merely nosed it under the door in front of him. When cook turned round the female rat had vanished so God knows where she is now and where she'll have her litter.'

'I didn't want to say anything before,' said Dora, 'but Professor Redhill does feel he is on the track of something that will do the trick. He's not, however, prepared to say anything until he has conclusive evidence that his new formula will work. He's a much chastened man since you last saw him, Prime Minister.'

'I should certainly hope so, Dora. I can see you have a much firmer grip on him than Bendigo ever had. Bendigo was too ready to give him whatever he asked for without insisting on some demonstration of progress.'

'That was Richard's way, I suppose,' said Dora, her voice mellow with understanding. 'I never thought he was really tough enough for the hurly-burly of political life.'

'Have you seen anything of him since he resigned his seat?'

'No, nor are we likely to for some time. He's in Albania.'

'Good God, has he defected? Why didn't someone tell me?'

'No Prime Minister, he hasn't defected. He's been appointed co-ordinator of an Anglo-Albanian film production. Actually, he's got himself involved with Clementina Carstairs.'

'That revolutionary woman you mean?'

'That's her.'

'But Bendigo was very much a middle-of-the-road man.'

'It's not the politics, it's the sex. With him anyway. With her it's the politics. She said she loved him because he was the only politician she had ever heard of who had resigned on a matter of principle.'

'Nonsense,' said the Prime Minister, 'there was – er, and . . . ' He thought. 'There have been a number,' he said at last. 'It's just that I can't remember their names.'

'Anyway, as far as Richard is concerned,' said Dora, 'he's supremely happy from all accounts. He has adored Clem for years but even apart from that he never in his wildest dreams expected to find a really beautiful woman offering him the kind of passionate adoration Clementina is capable of if someone strikes the right response in her. It's a wonderful new experience for him. He has always loved women but so far all those he has had have been pleasant and friendly ladies who have found him interesting and amusing and have gone to bed with him on that account, not being very much interested in sex themselves. Whereas Richard has always yearned for passion and glamour. Well he's got that all right even if Clementina isn't as young as she was, and now he's as happy as a ceratoid anglerfish.'

Dora's pleasure in the baffled look on the Prime Minister's face was in no way diminished by the fact that she was expecting it. She even knew what he was going to say and as he gasped out, 'a what?' she was already explaining.

'The ceratoid anglerfish,' she said, 'is a fish with a problem. For one thing there are very few of them about which is not surprising when you consider what happens when a male ceratoid anglerfish meets a female of the species.

'They live at depths of 500 metres or more in all the world's oceans which, anyway, are pretty indistinguishable from one another that far down. But being so widespread and so few in number they find it very difficult to find one another. So when they do meet it is not a case of fish that pass in the night or even wham, bam, thank you ma'am. In fact it couldn't be more for keeps than if they were devout Catholics married by the Pope. In the tips of the jaws of the male anglerfish there is a set of pincer-like teeth. Immediately on meeting a female he sinks them into her. He never, ever lets go. In the ensuing months he slowly fuses with his mate. It starts with the topmost layers of cells around the male's jaws. These become continuous with the corresponding female epidermis. Gradually the fusion becomes more extensive. Eventually, the two bodies are joined and the blood system connects. This means that the female eats for two and the male no longer needs to eat at all. But it doesn't finish there. He doesn't need his eyes so they virtually wither away; he doesn't need his digestive system so that goes. Eventually all the no longer needed organs atrophy; one only remains, the sole reason that the female is willing to go through all this discomfort. Her reward is that she has a constant supply of sperm on tap, as it were. His metamorphosis is into a pair of testes. They grow as the body shrinks until they come to occupy the whole of what remains of the male's body cavity. The two, once separate, fish stay like that for ever. Not even death parts them for they die simultaneously.'

'That is quite extraordinary, Dora,' said the Prime Minister. 'However did you get to know that?'

'I am Science Minister,' said Dora, smugly. 'I feel it is part of my work to know such matters.'

She did not think it necessary to add that it was Richard Bendigo himself who had told her the story of the ceratoid anglerfish over dinner one evening, years before.

'One thing only slightly puzzles me about your analogy between Richard and the extraordinary mating habits of this fish,' said the Prime Minister. 'Is it possible, if I may pose so indelicate a matter, that Bendigo could provide, as it were, sperm on tap?'

'I've no idea,' said Dora. 'But presumably he's enjoying allowing Clementina to find out. Incidentally, you do know what the word "ceratoid" means, Prime Minister?'

'I don't think I do, Dora. Please enlighten me.'

'Horny. It means having a hard, shell-like exterior or, as we usually put it, horny.'

'Science is a wonderful thing,' said the Prime Minister.

HM and Penny had had very little difficulty in getting into the Bletchley Camp but, like most of the people they had spent the last six months with, they were now anxious to get out. Security, however, was growing tighter every day. When the camp had first opened relationships between the immunees and the soldiers guarding them had been reasonably cordial. Most of the youngsters had been unemployed anyway – as had most of the soldiers which was why they had joined up – and had had no objection to the kind of life they had been asked to lead. Then the soldiers became envious, comparing their relatively disciplined life with the freedom and licence they witnessed in the camp itself. Some of the girls had, on principle, refused to sleep with the ones they were supposed to cohabit with and had, instead, made a dead set at the soldiers.

The rules became stricter. Any soldier found consorting with a camp girl was charged and, in the case of a repeated offence, sentenced to military detention. Once they realized that they were looked on as warders, the soldiers started to treat the immunees as prisoners. There was still a certain amount of sexual contact but the soldiers, instead of boasting about it to their friends, now tended to keep any liaison with a camp girl a secret. Violence, at first sporadic, became a regular occurrence. Lone soldiers were beaten up and then came retaliation by groups of soldiers on prisoners, not necessarily the ones who had been involved earlier, not necessarily even male prisoners. Complaints to the camp commandant, a civilian but a former brigadier, were met by a blanket refusal to accept complaints against the army. If visible injuries were produced as proof they were either dismissed as being caused by fights between the immunees themselves or, if soldiers could not possibly be eliminated, the immunees were told that they must stop their provocationary tactics and that they should be grateful for all that was being done for them. Would they prefer to be returned to ordinary life and the prospect of a useless, unproductive existence? Here at least they were engaged on activities of long-term benefit to this grand old country of theirs.

It was at this stage that HM and Penny, strolling arm in arm around the perimeter one cloudy afternoon, saw a white flash bounce off a grey wall and heard a familiar voice say: ‘C’m on man, just for the record now. Take me with these two.’

Freedom had handed his camera to a corporal and was already standing between HM and Penny, an arm around each waist. HM could feel the rough khaki through his thin shirt. 'Don't say anything now kids,' muttered Freedom. 'I'll see you tonight in the West Field.'

The West Field was a kind of no man's land where a certain amount of inter-sex fraternization was unofficially permitted on account of the thriving, prostitution-based black market which had given a number of the camp women – and some of the camp men – enough hard currency to buy goods from outside or to pay off anyone who was inclined to interrupt.

The commandant knew about it but was powerless to act. He was also disgusted. 'These people,' he told his wife, 'are supposed to be the inheritors of our world, the ones who will take over from us. But they've as many pimps and prostitutes in there as they have outside.' He tried to shake his head in sorrow and bewilderment but the chain wrapped around it and clipped to the brass bedrail hampered his movements. 'I'm ready now,' he said. 'You can start with the whip but this time increase the force slowly. Aaagh! That's wonderful.'

As Freedom squeezed their waists and waited, a smile splitting his face, for the corporal to take his photograph, HM whispered, 'Okay, but no camera. They'll lynch you if they think you're taking pictures there.'

'Don't worry,' said Freedom, 'leave it to me.'

That night they settled themselves into a corner of the field, deep in the long grass, and Freedom told them how Clementina had gone off to Albania with Richard Bendigo leaving him at a Total Art Environment peopled only by a few elderly hippies. 'All the kids have gone man,' he said, 'most of them here. Most are in the camp; some are in the army. And there's more rats than ever. At least the Pied Piper guy got rid of the rats before he took away the kids.'

He had taken the logical course, he said. Not being an immunee he had opted for the army. Dora, he said, had promised to help him get into the Army Photographic

Unit but so far the only thing that had come of it was a promise that eventually he would go on a course which would teach him how to use a camera the army way.

HM had a thought. 'If,' he said, lying at full length, his head on Freedom's haversack, 'if those kids are either in the camp or in the army, isn't there a good chance that half of those on the outside should be inside with us?'

'I would think more than half,' said Freedom.

'Then why the hell don't they join us?' asked Penny.

'Because,' said Freedom, 'they don't know. Did you know before they found out for you? There's no way they could find out. Few of them have been anywhere near the IG gases and those who have have always worn gas-masks.'

'That's no problem,' said Penny. 'It's easy to find out who's an immunee and who isn't; immunees taste different.'

'They what!'

'They taste different. At least that's what some of the girls say. Not only different but better.'

'You mean . . . '

'Sure. I mean three dots. I also mean that when you suck off an immunee he tastes different than an ordinary guy. All the girls say so. And some of the fellers. And some of the fellers say the same about the girls. And – '

'And some of the girls say the same about the girls I suppose,' broke in Freedom.

'That's right. We taste different. Everybody says so. All those who fool around at any rate. Not everyone does you know. I mean take us – I just stick to old HM here and he always tastes good. I've forgotten what it was like with anyone else, even you Freedom.'

Freedom gave a long, low whistle. 'You know kid,' he said to HM, 'if you organize it on the inside I'll organize it on the outside. There's going to be no shortage of guys willing to take the test. If I'm right and there are just as many immunees outside the wire as there are inside they won't have enough left in uniform to hold you here. You'll be able to walk out as soon as you please. No soldier's going to stop his own kind, even if he hasn't actually joined you himself.'

Freedom rose to his feet and picked up the haversack HM had been resting his head on. 'Come on,' he said, giving it to Penny, 'just one.'

Penny pushed it away. 'Are you crazy?' she said. 'They'll kill us.'

'They won't know,' said Freedom. 'It's the latest army equipment, an infra-red camera. I got sick of waiting for them to send me on the course so I took a trip up there myself and borrowed it to practise on. Some of them have come out real nice. Come on kid, just one.'

'That's right kid,' a woman's voice giggled in the darkness. 'Give him one, just one like he said. That's all they can bleedin' do anyway.'

Chapter 10

The Prime Minister had adjourned the Cabinet meeting so that they could all see the news on television and they swivelled their straight-backed chairs round so that they could watch the screen on the wall at the far end of the room. The pictures were not very exciting, a long stream of cheerful youngsters shambling along waving banners which evidently had been hastily prepared for in some cases poster paint had been used and had run. They were flanked by a discreet escort of mounted policemen and were watched by groups of silent onlookers on the pavement. From the marchers came the confused and raggedy hum of shuffling feet and voices, periodically broken by an attempt at a shouted slogan which lost its energy and tailed away by the time those behind realized that it had started.

'Surely they're not just letting them march here like that, unimpeded,' gasped the Minister Without Portfolio.

'What do you expect us to do?' snapped the Prime Minister. 'Shoot them down in full view of their watching mothers and fathers? Baton charge them? It's not strictly speaking even a political demonstration which might have given us some justification. Many of them, in fact, are our own members and supporters.'

'But surely Prime Minister, the IG gases obviated the necessity for such – er – forceful tactics.'

The Prime Minister's look would have withered an ordinary man. 'It seems altogether to have slipped your mind, Minister, that the only effect of IG gases on that lot would be to immobilize the onlookers. As they are already passive to the point of stagnation there would hardly be any purpose in doing that. Also, the gases would freeze the horses and that would be both pointless and unpopular with the television viewers. The marchers would then be able to continue on their way without impediment.'

'But they're being unimpeded anyway, Prime Minister.'

'My dear chap, you must have patience. I am about to tell you what, very shortly, you will have to accept your share of Cabinet responsibility for. The marchers will be allowed into Trafalgar Square and then down Whitehall – to both of which the general public has already been denied access. They will be stopped at the corner of Downing Street but their leaders will then be allowed to present a petition to the Cabinet here, already in session to discuss their claims – and sympathetically inclined. The cameras will watch the petitioners being courteously received here at the door by officials and invited in. There will then be a most unfortunate accident.'

'We're going to shoot the buggers,' asked the Minister of Education hopefully.'

'I mean,' said the Prime Minister, 'that there will be most unfortunate accident to the television cameras – the mobile generator will blow up.'

'But that will only account for one lot of cameras, Prime Minister.'

'That's all right Home Secretary; the other lot will be too concerned photographing their rivals' distress to notice what else is going on.'

'What else will be going on?'

'As the ringleaders are brought into the hall downstairs a squad of policemen will emerge from the cellars and arrest them, returning them to the cellars and holding them there until the situation is clear enough for them to be taken to a more secure place. At the same time a combined unit of military and civilian police, at this moment concealed in the Home Office – I am sorry

Home Secretary but you could not be informed of this in advance, a matter of security as I am sure you would be the first to appreciate – this combined force will emerge from the Home Office and proceed to – er – buffet the crowd into dispersal. If there is any indication that the other television cameras are not entirely occupied with their colleagues' misfortune they will be quickly overturned by a number of plain-clothes men who are thoroughly experienced in acting as a riotous mob. They have already infiltrated the marchers.

'Certainly, the Bletchley business has not turned out as we planned but we have a register of everyone who was there and I have asked the Minister of Science to come up with a more practical method of dealing with the situation than was advanced by her predecessor. I must say I feel at liberty now to confess something that, at the time, was noted only in my political diary – and that is that I had my doubts all along about Bendigo's proposals for dealing with the immunees, indeed I had thought for some time that he was not up to the responsibilities I had placed on his shoulders. Which is why, as you no doubt realize now, I eventually had to ask him to resign.'

'But Prime Minister – '

'Sorry Foreign Secretary, but if you don't mind I think we should all hear what the commentator is saying.'

'Ten thousand immunees from their centre near Bletchley broke out of their camp last night and started marching towards London. There was no violence. Earlier reports suggested that for several days girls in the camp had been urging young soldiers, most of them aged between 18 and 22, to take a simple test they had devised which would indicate if they too were immune from the effects of the Incapacitating Gases, an infallible sign of genetic change. It is estimated that more than two-thirds found they were so immune. Most of them threw away their arms, changed into civilian clothes and joined their fellow immunees. A psychologist explained that it was natural for all species to seek the company of their own kind. As a result, when the immunees decided to leave camp in the early hours of this morning there were not enough guards to contain them. A spokesman for the immunees said that a rally would be held in Trafalgar Square and that a petition will be presented to the Prime Minister demanding the right to live in pairs after a religious ceremony. One splinter-group of right-wing protestors want to make it a capital offence to have a child out of wedlock. Others are pressing for birth control and abortion facilities, neither of which was available at Bletchley. All of them demand the right to cohabit with anyone, regardless of whether they are immune or not. This will mean a repeal of Section Two of the recently passed Propagation Act. A Downing Street spokesman said – '

The Prime Minister pressed his control button and the screen went blank. 'I don't suppose any of us wants to hear what a Downing Street spokesman said,' he observed. 'And besides, I think I can hear them coming.'

He rose from his chair and went to the window overlooking Downing Street. A number of ministers, including Dora, grouped around him.

'It's always the same with this God-forsaken country,' said the Justice Minister. 'The moment you give them what they want they want something else. Or they want two incompatible things at the same time. Why can't they do what's best for them?'

There was the sound of distant chanting which became louder and clearer when Dora threw open the window and leaned out.

'They've stopped on the corner,' she said. 'And there's a group coming here. I can't make out who they are.'

The crowd behind them chanted: 'NO PROMISCUITY!'

'ONE MAN, ONE WIFE!'

'TAKE HEED, DON'T BREED!'

Then there was a chant of 'Two, four six, eight, we're not going to propagate.'

To which another section of the crowd responded with a roar of: 'Two, four, six, eight, better far to masturbate.'

There was another chant which no one could hear properly. Dora leaned as far out as she could, the Prime Minister putting a restraining hand on her back. Dora, once she was aware that it was his hand, found it strangely thrilling. The idea of power as an aphrodisiac was not new to her but this was the first indication she had that it could also be a sexual catalyst. For the first time for many years a faint frisson of heterosexual lubricity flickered across her mind and lodged fleetingly in her body itself. 'Fancy that,' she thought in amazement. 'How could I fancy that?' All the same, she made no move to escape from the pressure of the Prime Minister's hand on the small of her back.

'Can you make out what they're chanting now, Dora?' he asked.

'Hold on a tick, Prime Minister, yes, I think I've got it – higomous, hogamous, we are monogamous – hogamous, higamous, the PM's polygamous.'

'Nonsense,' snapped the Prime Minister. 'Come away and shut the window Dora. It's not dignified for us to stand here. Anyway, I've never looked at another woman in all the years I've been married to whatsername. Come away Dora.'

'One moment Prime Minister, it looks as if they're having trouble holding the crowd.'

'Of course they are; they're out of practice. Most haven't done it for years and some never at all.'

'It's all right,' said Dora. 'The army's there now; they've formed a double cordon. And what's more there's a row of soldiers behind them with their guns pointing at the crowd.'

'That's right, like I said, shoot the buggers,' said the Minister for Education.

'It's only a show of force,' said the Prime Minister. 'I've given strict orders that there must be no shooting. Close the window now Dora.'

His hand left the small of her back caressingly. I wonder, he thought, what it would be like with a Lesbian.

The noise outside was muffled but not muffled enough to disguise the unmistakable rattle of gunfire. Dora was first at the window again. As she threw it open the noise of the automatic fire sharpened and invaded the room like bees, hurling itself against the glass of the portraits, burying itself in the velvet drapes and furniture. Acrid cordite wreathed through the open window and a spent bullet bounced off the toughened glass above Dora's head. Everyone had dived to the floor and rolled behind furniture or under the table. Only the Prime Minister stood at the window, his arm by now around Dora's waist.

'You must stop the killing, Prime Minister,' said a frightened voice from behind the sofa. 'It will lead to revolution.'

'It's all right,' said Dora. 'They're firing away from the crowd, not at them. They're firing at the rats, more rats than I've ever seen before. The street is full of them. Now the crowd's running and so are the police and soldiers.'

The firing was spluttering to a halt and its place was being filled by screams and shouts. Below that was a constant sibilant shrilling, a scattering, scampering sound that seemed to crawl up the stonework of the old building and squeak through gaps in the crumbling mortar.

'It's horrible,' said Dora, pressing herself up against the Prime Minister for the warmth and comfort of another body. 'They're pulling people down, biting them. It's dreadful.'

'Come away Dora, we can do nothing for the moment,' said the Prime Minister in a voice gentler than she would have ever thought possible. 'Our work is not in the streets but above the battle.'

'Wait,' she said, 'look who's just turned the corner. Isn't it Professor Redhill? Oh look at him Prime Minister, just look at him. He's waving that rat around his head almost as if it were a banner. Now he's let go and picked up another before the first one has even hit the wall. Now he's doing the same with the second. Look at his other hand; he's holding a piece of paper. He's seen us! He's waving and shouting something. I can't make it out. Yes I can! He's shouting, "I've got it, I've got it!" It's the formula! It must be the formula!'

Dora was dancing up and down.

'My God he's laying about him now, kicking them, hitting them. They seem to be making for him, groups of them from the other side of the road, running from the other end of the street, running towards him, climbing on him. Oh my God he's down. Quick PM, the binoculars.'

Without waiting she snatched a pair of binoculars that were on a side table near the window and rapidly focused on the still struggling figure, the hand grasping the paper now held high. 'Quick,' she snapped, 'get this down somebody – KOH (aq) plus Ca (Oh) 2 plus MH4 CN plus – oh damn, he's gone.'

'Gone! What the hell do you mean, gone?' The Prime Minister snatched the binoculars from her and fumbled to alter the focus.

'Fuck it,' he cried, 'I can't get the fucking thing focused. It's all fucking blurred.'

'It's no use Prime Minister,' said Dora, turning away from the window. 'The rats will have eaten it by now. And Professor Redhill too, for that matter. We'll just have to start all over again.'

* * *

George, ejected from the cellar by the heavy-booted men, desperate like the rest of the tribe for a place where he could rest undisturbed in the daylight hours, had been followed into the street by all the neighbouring ratclans. The gunfire and the smell of blood excited and stimulated them all but George had been content to play only a peripheral role in the street fighting; that is until his sharp eyes spotted Professor Redhill coming round the corner. It was George who had led the charge across the street, George who, somehow, had signalled to the others to concentrate on the Professor as he struggled to reach Number 10. And it was George who had pulled him down, George whose sharp, pointed teeth had first ripped into the piece of paper in the Professor's hand, George whose eye had turned mercilessly on to the still-conscious eye that peered out of the blood-spattered face, George who went for the throat.

Chapter 11

They ran steadily, not knowing where they were running except that it was away from the rats, the gunfire, the police, the soldiers and, as the crowds thinned out, even from the others, their own kind. Except, of course, that Freedom, jogging along easily on the other side of Penny, was not one of their own kind, being made up of unevolved genes, or at least genes that had decided they had had enough of evolution for the time being. And yet Freedom was closer to them than some of the people they had met in the camp at Bletchley and who were immunees like themselves. Their new genes had not been of much help to them; they had certainly not made them any happier. They had been frightened at the idea of being different from their families, had been unable to adapt to the changed emotional map of their lives just as the others, those still outside, were deprived of the ability to adapt to a changed physical environment. They had been miserable, some losing themselves to drink, sex or the drugs that had soon become readily available; others had become vicious.

'The only way we're different,' Penny had said one night, 'is that we can breathe bad air. That doesn't necessarily make us either better people or better at doing things. I don't even know whether we are an advance on previous life forms, a backward step on the way to something more primitive that will eventually sink into some post-holocaust ooze or an error, a sideways slip up a blind alley. All I do know is that we had nothing to do with how we got here and that we'll have even less to say in how it's going to work out.'

That had been weeks ago and now here she was, jogging by his side, looking lithe and beautiful, sweat dampening her face, running in rivulets down her neck. She noticed HM was looking at her and smiled.

'We were lucky to get out of that little lot,' she said.

'Save your breath Penny,' Freedom said, 'we've got a long way to go yet till we're clear. That's if there's such a place as clear, man.'

'Just where are we going,' asked HM. 'Any ideas?'

'East,' said HM. 'And as we're heading this way we might just as well keep on heading this way.'

'I think I'll have to stop soon,' said Penny.

'Stop,' said Freedom. 'Just what's the matter with you, kid? You're younger than I am – you're even younger than HM here. You're fit, you're strong. You can keep on going for miles. Just like little old Freedom here. Come on, I want a picture of me running like this. That'll give 'em something to think about in Nebraska or wherever that goddam university is.'

He handed the camera to HM who veered slightly to one side so that he could get Freedom in the view-finder.

'That's all very well,' said Penny. 'But you're not having a baby.'

All three stopped and HM handed the camera back to Freedom. 'I think all there is on that one is a patch of sky,' he said. 'How long have you known?'

'About ten minutes, I guess,' said Penny. 'I've had so much on my mind this last week or so that I just didn't notice the signs. Then as we were running I got to thinking, and once I got to thinking I got to feeling sick and that's when I told you. I've not been keeping anything back.'

They looked around. They were in a windswept expanse of concrete surrounded by tall towers that had been abandoned long ago. Two of the cluster of six had collapsed and, in the gathering darkness, they could just make out the more orderly rubble of blocks that had been deliberately pulled down.

'Any ideas where we are?' asked HM.

'I can just make out an old sign over there. BARB something,' said Freedom.

'It doesn't matter,' said HM. 'The main thing is to find shelter before it gets dark. This place will be full of rats.'

'Not up there man,' said Freedom, pointing to the top of the nearest tower. 'The more it sways the less they like it. You don't find rats above the fifteenth floor of any of these blocks. They're too nervous.'

'You don't find people there either,' said Penny, 'but I don't suppose we have much choice. There's nowhere else is there?'

They climbed 25 flights before they found something habitable. There was a door that was locked and Freedom reasoned that if it was locked something worthwhile might be beyond it. At least it would not have been vandalized. When he eventually got the door open the setting sun shining through the window showed them a room with a carpet, a table and a sofa. Next door was a bed and a wardrobe which still contained a few clothes.

'I don't suppose we'll do better than this,' said HM, 'so we might as well stop here. For the time being anyway.'

'How will we get food and water up here?' asked Penny.

'Don't worry about that kid,' said Freedom. 'We'll see to that in the morning. We'll work something out.'

But Penny hadn't heard him. She had opened the glass door on to the balcony and was looking out on to the vast, battered panorama of London. The sun was low on the horizon, red from the millions of particles of pollutants that hung in the air and distorted its rays. But all the three of them saw was its beauty.

'If you lean out over the balcony and look round the corner,' said Penny, 'you can see St Paul's.'

'You'd better be careful kid,' said Freedom. 'Those balcony rails can't be too safe.'

'I'm not a fool,' said Penny. 'I don't lean on anything until I've tested it out.'

'Or anyone?' asked HM.

Penny considered. 'That's right,' she said eventually. 'The people I lean on have been tried and tested and turned out to be true.'

She shivered in the rapidly cooling air.

Inside the flat, Freedom said: 'What we need is food, light and drink and I'm going to get all three. Sitting here hungry in the dark is not a good way to live.'

He was back within two hours and they eagerly ate the cold pub food which was all he had been able to get in that area at that hour. Their faces glowed in the light of the candle he had persuaded the pub manager to lend him. Afterwards all three of them sat on the bed, the one blanket they had found in the wardrobe around their shoulders. Freedom opened the bottle of whisky he had bought and passed it round. After a while he got off the bed to blow the candle out. So it was he who noticed the other lights. Penny and HM went to the window to look. All round them in the surrounding tower blocks tiny flickers of light, some candleglow, others the stab of an electric torch, were to be seen.

'So there are others living like this,' whispered Penny. 'I wonder if they're immunees too.'

'It doesn't matter, does it,' said HM. 'The main thing is that they are there. It means you'll get help when you have the baby.'

'The baby? Up here?'

'The place has been standing for fifty or sixty years so it should last out another few. When the baby starts to walk we'll find somewhere else. But there's plenty of time. It gives us some breathing space. We'll survive.'

They were lying down now, all three under the blanket.

Every now and again one of them sat up to take a swig of the Scotch.

'What we've got to do,' said Freedom, 'is to figure out some way of getting supplies up here. Otherwise it'll kill us. It'll have to be some kind of pulley and basket from the balcony.'

'It's a long way down,' said HM.

'It's a longer way up,' said Freedom.

'What we need,' said Penny sleepily, 'is a place where they've suspended the laws of gravity.'

'Physics is physics, the whole universe over,' said HM. 'They won't suspend the laws of gravity for our benefit. We'll have to use ingenuity instead.'

'I don't see any reason why they can't suspend any law they want to,' said Freedom. 'If evolution is on the move again anything can happen. Who knows what your kid's going to be like for a start. Hey man, do you think he could have wings?'

'You want him to fly up with the groceries?' asked Penny.

'No,' said Freedom, 'it's just that anything can happen, the universe is more complicated than its name suggests. It should be called the diverse.'

'All I was saying,' said Penny, 'is that there is anti-matter – or so they say – so why shouldn't there be anti-gravity as well? Maybe it's the same thing. What we need is a place which repelled instead of attracted, a place where any object that wasn't nailed down simply disappeared into the sky. That way all we would need to do is to use the empty lift shaft and the groceries would come hurtling up. At least,' she added, 'that would save my wonderful winged baby from being used as an errand boy – or girl.'

There was a longer silence. Then Freedom said: 'I once worked in a place like that.'

'Like what?' said HM.

'A place that repelled everybody. And where the laws of gravity were suspended. They not only chained the typewriters to the desks, they chained the desks to the floor. Everything that wasn't nailed down or chained down disappeared. A pencil might last a day but they never got the ball-point pens out of the cardboard box.

'Once the manager came round at the end of the week and said that so much stuff had been nicked that they had worked out that we not only had had our wages in kind but actually owed the company an additional £10. Of course we got very indignant and threatened strike action unless the imputation was withdrawn immediately, so they did. All the same, some of the lads were ready to compromise and settle for a fiver.

'Haven't I told you that one before?'

There was no answer, only the soft breath of sleep.

Freedom slipped out from under the blanket and felt for his infra-red camera. He could see HM and Penny, their faces close to each other, by the light of the stars filtering through the grimy but uncurtained window. He took his picture and went back to bed.

'Life's gotta go on,' he muttered as he too fell asleep.